WE ARE THE PEOPLE

Our Parents Warned Us About

A JAKE SULLIVAN NOVEL

CHIP BELL

THE JAKE SULLIVAN SERIES

Come Monday

Trying to Reason with Hurricane Season

Havana Daydreamin'

A Pirate Looks at Forty

One Particular Harbour

Son of a Son of a Sailor

Jamaica Mistaica

Changes in Latitudes, Changes in Attitudes

He Went to Paris

Tampico Trauma

Fins

Big Rig

We Are The People Our Parents Warned Us About

ALSO AVAILABLE

Trilogy

The First Ten Adventures

COMING SPRING 2019

Cuban Crime of Passion

WE ARE THE PEOPLE
Our Parents Warned Us About

A JAKE SULLIVAN NOVEL

CHIP BELL

Copyright ©2018 by Chip Bell

All rights reserved. No part of this book/manuscript may be reproduced in any form or by any electronic or mechanical means, including information or storage and retrieval systems, without permission in writing from the author.

Printed in the United States of America.

"I was supposed to have been a Jesuit priest or a Naval Academy grad."

– "WE ARE THE PEOPLE OUR PARENTS
WARNED US ABOUT"
BY JIMMY BUFFETT

DEDICATION

To Parrotheads everywhere, who do good works, have great fun, and who allow me to be a small part of the craziness!

ACKNOWLEDGEMENT

To all those members of Parrotheads in Paradise, Inc., and the Trop Rock family who allowed me to mention them in this book.

PROLOGUE

PROLOGUE

CHAPTER 1

"*Everything has changed,*" thought Jake Sullivan, as he lay in the rain on the flagstones of Mallory Square. He knew he had been shot, and the pain in his shoulder made it difficult for him to lift his head, but he heard the feet coming toward him, splashing in the puddles, as the steady tap of a cane struck the stones. He blinked away the rain and focused and saw his enemy standing over him.

"I told you, Jake Sullivan . . . I told you I would come for you . . . and here I am . . ."

THE PRESIDENT

CHAPTER 2

The flashes of the emergency vehicle lights somehow pierced his closed eyelids and a kaleidoscope of images raced back and forth, alternating with periods of total darkness. Jake felt wet and cold and heard sounds, and then the movie would start again.

Jordan Fletcher had finished his second term with the highest approval rating in history – 65 percent – better than Ronald Reagan's 63 percent. His handpicked successor, his Vice President, Franklin Turner, a former U.S. Senator from Pennsylvania, and his running mate, Martin Polanco, a Florida Governor and son of a Cuban real estate mogul, who had fled Castro and lived the American dream, won the election in a landslide, promising more of the "Fletcher Way".

THE FRIEND

CHAPTER 3

Jake remembered the discussions they all had and suddenly he was in the Oval Office with a hand-picked group of people from the administration, who were determining what they would do after Fletcher's Presidency.

All agreed that the group Fletcher had formed to protect the country was too important and needed to be maintained, and Turner gave his blessing to the idea, knowing that the threat of Group 45 and other entities still existed, and he needed people who could work, in private, and handle situations in which the government could not openly become involved.

Jake said the name to himself, "*FSI, Fletcher Security and Investigations*". A private firm . . . a group of people Fletcher hand-picked from the team who had populated his administration and other people he trusted and depended upon, was formed, in concept, a year before he left office.

His first two picks were Jake Sullivan and Mike Lang.

Jake's head ached and the light continued to come and go . . . and then there was Mike Lang, his colleague and best friend, and their conversation was rewinding on the tape that kept running, on and off, as he slipped deeper into darkness.

"So what do you think about all this?" asked Mike.

"What can I say? I'm honored, but I don't know how Linda's going to take this. I made a promise to her, and if I do this, it's a promise I have to break."

"It's a tough choice, my friend," said Mike, shaking his head. "I know how much you love your family, but I also know how much you love your country. I also know Jake Sullivan, and I know how hard it is for him to walk away when the job isn't done, when the threat still exists, when the bad guys are still out there."

"I know, Mike," said Jake, "and you're right, but Linda and the girls have given up a lot for me for a long time, and to ask them to do this again . . . it's not fair to them, and if I do this, it could destroy everything we have."

"Just know this, my friend," said Mike, putting his hand on Jake's shoulder, "whatever you decide, I'm with you, and I'll back you . . . now go home and talk to Linda."

CHAPTER 4

Jake remembered that weeks and months had passed, and he and Mike continued to talk it out.

He hadn't brought it up with Linda or his daughters yet. He wanted to wait until he had all the details as to where they would be located and exactly what his job description would be, but all the while, he knew two things deep down inside: that whatever it was, he was going to take the position . . . and it was irretrievably going to damage his relationship with Linda and the girls.

Mike had been right. He just couldn't walk away. Group 45 was still out there, and he knew, no matter what any of the others thought, Group 45 was behind it all, and they were inside the government and had to be rooted out. They had to be crushed once and for all and, call it ego or whatever you wanted, Jake knew he was the only one who could do it.

It drove him. It consumed him. And like the hero in a Greek tragedy, he couldn't help himself. He had to be part of the fight, no matter the cost.

He remembered Mike coming to him and telling him that he had great news ... that Charlotte Kosior had been given the

position of Director of Native American Artifacts at the Smithsonian, and that they had found a place in Georgetown close to where FSI would be headquartered in Washington.

Mike had been named Chief Investigator, a position he surely deserved, and Jake remembered his happiness and excitement, and he remembered when he and Linda were young and when they had all their dreams and the future lay open before them without any restrictions and without any fears.

The pain in Jake's head was increasing, and the periods of darkness began to outweigh the periods of light, but he could see himself in the Oval Office, just he and Jordan Fletcher, after everyone else had gone.

"It has to be you, Jake," said Fletcher, "no one else can take this job. I need you to do this. You will be Chief of Operations of the whole company, overseeing everything.
Given our technology, you can maintain your home in Miami ... in fact, I prefer you in that sphere of operations, given your knowledge of the area," said Fletcher, as he arose from behind the Resolute Desk and stared out the elongated windows of the Oval Office.
"I'm honored, Mr. President," said Jake, "but I have to run this past my family."
Fletcher never turned around.

"I understand your situation, Jake. I know what's occurred between you and Linda in the past because of this job. It's called sacrifice, son ... sacrifice for your country, and, quite frankly, a sacrifice for me." He turned and stared at Jake. "I hope it's a sacrifice you're willing to make, because as far as I'm concerned, there's no one else who can do this job."

Jake remembered thinking, "Mike and I ... best friends ... looking at a future where things suddenly diverge ... where Mike begins a new portion of his life ... and where I fear a portion of mine will end."

THE WIFE

CHAPTER 5

There were new sounds ... more people talking. Jake could sense that the rain had ended, but he was still wet and cold. Time didn't matter. Night ... day ... he couldn't tell ... seconds or hours. He had no knowledge of it passing, but then he thought ... he thought he heard a voice ... Linda!

He remembered the day she moved back to Pennsylvania.

Jake and Linda had always agreed, when he left government service, they would move back to Pennsylvania and he would enter into the private practice of law, and they would spend time with their family. Their daughter, Jennifer, had given birth to their first grandchild, Danny, and Jessica had married and planned to start a family, and Linda looked forward to being with them and doing all the things grandparents do.

Then one day Jake came home and explained about FSI and what Fletcher had asked of him. Jake tried to explain that Group 45 was still out there and he had to see it through. He had to take the fight to them. He had to make sure they were rooted out and destroyed, and only then would he feel that the country, his friends, and his family were safe. They argued.

"Why you, Jake? Why always you? This has become an obsession with you. You think you're the only person that can do this."

"Maybe I am," replied Jake. "Maybe I'm the only one who has the ability to do this, and the President needs me."

"He's not going to be the President anymore," snapped Linda, "but you've chosen him once again over us. We have given so much throughout this entire thing. I accepted who you were, who you are, and what you do . . . well, not this time! You've done remarkable service for him and the country . . . but you can't give it up. It's you . . . not him! And that, I can't and will not accept! We have two wonderful children and now a grandchild, and still you choose this life of danger and death. I just can't Jake. I can't . . . and I won't . . . not this time."

CHAPTER 6

"It all happened so fast," thought Jake.

Linda was gone, their house in Miami was sold, and Jake, having resigned from the Department of Justice, found himself staying at the Pier House Resort in Key West. He had chosen Key West as the place where he would live, at least temporarily, because it was the one place where he could find some peace where all the things pulling at him seemed to ease up a little bit, where he could cut the strings, pull his thoughts together, and determine what he should do.

He had kept the property on Whitehead, where his former office and apartment had been located before the bombing by Benjamin Matthews's crew, and FSI was building him a new office on the site with all the latest bells and whistles as to communications, technology, and security.

Eva had agreed to come with him, and he was even able to rehire his old handyman, Hector Sanchez. He also had demanded that Sam Walsh have an office in the building for tech support. Fletcher readily agreed and Sam was made the Chief of Technology for the entire company, much to his delight.

Until then, Jake lived at the resort of his own choosing, and FSI had rented condos for Eva and Sam until more permanent residences could be obtained.

Jake remembered meeting them as they arrived at the airport in Key West.

    Eva hugged him especially tight, knowing what had happened with Linda. She looked up at him.
    "Are you sure about this?"
    "I know, Eva. I may be wrong, but it's what I have to do."
    "You'll get through it. At some point it will end, and when it does, your family will come back to you."
    "We'll see," said Jake. "I hope you're right, but..."

CHAPTER 7

The scene before Jake changed.

He had flown out of that same airport to Pittsburgh. His youngest daughter, Jessica, had flown in from Dallas with her husband, Brett, and Jennifer and her husband, Jason, and Danny, who lived near Linda and her newly purchased home, all came together to hear Jake's plea for understanding and to explain why he had to do what he had to do.

Jake had prosecuted many cases in Federal Court, and like it is with most juries, it wasn't the facts that prevailed, it was the emotion.

He had hurt their mother . . . hurt them . . . he had chosen work and duty over family, based upon his obsession with his enemy. He could do nothing in the end but apologize . . . tell them how much he loved them, and that he'd make sure they were safe.

The hugs from his daughters when he went to leave gave him some comfort, but Linda simply turned and left the room as he said his goodbyes.

His betrayal to her was still too raw, still too deep, and she couldn't accept the choice he had made, and he understood, and for the briefest of moments, he thought of giving it all up, but then he looked at his grandson, Danny, and held him. He knew he had to do what he was going to do for him and for all of them.

He kissed his girls and his grandson goodbye, shook the hands of his sons-in-law, and walked out the door, wondering if he would ever be able to fully come back to the family he loved so dearly.

THE STAFF

CHAPTER 8

After several months of expedited work, Jake's office on Whitehead was completed. The first floor had a reception area where Eva would work, there was a separate tech center for Sam, and Jake's office took up most of the back. It was part office and part conference room, where a crisis team could be assembled when necessary.

Jake had requested an apartment above the office, but this time, there were two stairways: external and internal . . . known only to Jake . . . one of the security measures that Fletcher had insisted upon for the building. Others included cameras, sensors, sound systems, and secret compartments where armaments were stored. The building had been reinforced to withstand all but the most explosive firepower, and all the windows were high grade bulletproof glass.

FSI had purchased the rented condos for both Sam and Eva, a short walk from the office. Given the newness of the place and the way it had been designed and completed, there wasn't much for a handyman to do, and Hector found himself being more of an errand boy and cleaning man than anything else.

Jake had never found Hector to be especially warm. He had a hard life in Cuba and had worked at odd jobs his whole life, both there and since he came to the United States. He kept to himself a great deal, but he was close to Eva, and Jake sensed that in a crisis, he would be one of the first people he could truly depend upon.

Jake had called everybody in once the office was up and running, and Joe Toliver from FSI gave them a lecture about the facility and all its bells and whistles.

After he left, and while everyone was still assembled in the conference room, Jake looked at each of them, hands on his hips, and said, "Well, the boredom is over. Let's get up and running, and let's get to work." And without a word, they all did.

THE ISLAND

CHAPTER 9

Key West was alive. The effects of Hurricane Irma lingered, but the pall that hung over things had dissipated. The damage to the island hadn't been that severe, but there were some buildings that had been battered, trees that had been toppled, and the streets had been coated with mud and debris, but the spirit of the people never faded. The fear that had kept tourists from coming to the island, due to grossly exaggerated news reports of damage, seemed to be mostly gone. The cruise ships were docking and the streets were crowded. Music filled Duval Street, and the art works, sights, and sounds of the island were blooming.

Jake spent a lot of time inside the office and in the apartment. He would stop in occasionally at the Schooner Wharf in the afternoon to catch Mike McCloud, get lunch at B.O.'s Fish Wagon, or order Cuban sandwiches from El Siboney, and stop in at the Chart Room on occasion to converse with the locals.

He spoke to his girls at least once a week. But his conversations with Linda were limited to financial matters and other details that they needed to agree on. As time passed, he sensed a softening and a lessening of Linda's anger, but he never broached the subject of reconciliation, and neither did she.

For now, at least, he considered Key West his home. The island was his base of operations, and as time went on, he became more and more comfortable, as he had before, and he found peace and enjoyment there, all the while still being consumed by the job he had chosen.

THE JOB

CHAPTER 10

Jake felt himself being lifted. He felt it before. Somehow the lights that came and went before him seemed brighter, but he couldn't tell for sure. He remembered the bright lights in the conference room at FSI headquarters in Washington, the meetings with Fletcher and Mike and the others.

Headquarters were in Washington, D.C., but other office sites had been created in New York, Los Angeles, Seattle, Atlanta, and Chicago. Although FSI handled all types of investigations, its main reason for existence was still the hunt for Group 45 and its new presumed leader, Ortiz. There had only been rumors of sightings and chatter had been kept to a minimum. The paperwork had to be reviewed. There could be no chance that something was missed, but, for lack of a better word, Jake had found it all to be boring. He needed to move. He needed some excitement. He needed a challenge. And most of all, he needed to find Ortiz . . . and then, one day . . .

THE CHALLENGE

CHAPTER 11

It came. Jake remembered it. The excitement . . . he could feel it . . . the challenge he had waited for. He couldn't quite remember now. Thoughts were fuzzy, timing uncertain . . . six months, seven months, more?

He remembered some successes. Foiling a kidnapping in Somalia, stopping an assassination in Tel Aviv . . . and a terrorist attack in Brussels . . . but there had been no major operations against Group 45. They had heard chatter that a ruling committee of the group was being formed, and they were certain that Ortiz had been or was going to be named the head, but again, the chatter was minimal and there had been no obvious acts by the group for quite some time . . . and nothing that could be considered a notification of such a meeting . . . and then things changed.

CHAPTER 12

Jake didn't know why, but the pain had gone away. The movie in his head seemed to be playing at a slower pace, but some things were distinct, even though others were not.

He remembered, it was a Tuesday morning when he came down to the office, just as Sam Walsh rushed in, throwing his laptop on his desk and motioning for Jake to follow him into tech support.

"I got something early this morning that might prove interesting."

Jake remembered his senses becoming more alert.

"What have you got, Sam?"

Sam sat down at the computer, his fingers flying over the keyboard, images appearing on the screens.

"This was hidden in a bunch of otherwise unimportant chatter."

Jake looked at the screen, which read, *"Cuban take out. Pier House. Next Saturday."*

Jake looked at Sam.

"Sounds like a dinner date to me."

"It could, except for one thing. Next Saturday, the 30th high school reunion for Key West High School is being held at the Pier House."

"And why are we interested in a high school reunion?" asked Jake.

"Because one of the graduates is now Vice President of the United States."

THE
VICE PRESIDENT

CHAPTER 13

Jake remembered when he had first been introduced to Martin Polanco, a tall, dark-haired, extremely handsome young man. He had been born and grown up in Key West. His parents had fled Cuba and come to the United States years before, and his father had gotten in on the early boom in Key West real estate and had made a fortune. He had sent his son to Harvard and bankrolled his political campaigns, leading to the Governorship of the State of Florida.

Polanco seemed like a good man to Jake. He wanted to continue opening up relations with Cuba to fight the epidemic of crime that was sweeping over the homeland of his parents. Many of the other leaders in the Cuban community in Miami and elsewhere opposed this policy since President Tianto was still running a Castro-like regime on the island, but President Fletcher was a proponent of the same policy, and given the Electoral College, Polanco's credentials, and his background, Fletcher, who had always been politically savvy, knew that if there was any doubt as to whether or not his legacy would continue, the Electoral votes of Pennsylvania and Florida, with their favorite sons on the ballot, would be hard to beat.

CHAPTER 14

"Would you like to find out where this thing originated?" asked Sam. "I know it looks like it came from Key West, but I tracked it. It originated in Cuba, went through the Balkans, then the Mid-East, and arrived on a 'Happenings in Key West' site."

Jake stared at the screen... *"Take out... assassination?"* and his juices started flowing.

"Eva!" he yelled out to the reception area, "get a video conference set up with everybody!"

"What's up, boss?" she asked.

Jake turned and looked at the screen again and said, mostly to himself, "Not sure yet, but something tells me this is much, much more than a dinner date."

CHAPTER 15

Jake settled in behind his desk and switched on his computer screen and was connected with a conference room in Washington, where Mike and Jordan Fletcher sat, along with Jason Bates, who was still Fletcher's right-hand man.

Jake went over what Sam Walsh had provided.

"I can't prove it," he said, "but I think it's a credible threat."

"Why?" asked Fletcher.

"Look at the origination. Everything we know about Ortiz indicates he's still somewhere in Cuba, and look at the routing pattern."

Mike nodded.

"You're right. All hot spots for Group 45 activitiy."

"Does anyone have any doubts," asked Fletcher, looking around the room and then at Jake, "that Ortiz controls Tianto?"

"None whatsoever," said Bates. "Every piece of intel we've gotten indicates that's the case."

"Sounds like you might be onto something, Jake," said Fletcher.

"I'd like to ask you to send Mike down and let us work on it and see what we come up with."

"Mike?" asked Fletcher.

"Sounds like a plan to me. I'll catch the first plane out."

"There you have it, Jake. Be careful on this one. Polanco is a good man. I don't want to lose him. I'll coordinate things on my end with the Secret Service so you don't have any problems with territorial disputes when he gets there."

"Thank you, sir," said Jake.

Fletcher got up and left the room. Bates looked over at Mike and then stared from the screen at Jake.

"I'm really happy you two are getting back together, but you heard the President. Try not to lose the Vice President . . . and also not destroying the island would be a good idea."

Mike got up and walked past Bates on his way to the door and slapped him on the back.

"Come on, Jason, cheer up. When have we ever failed you?"

Bates watched as Mike left and turned again to face Jake, who was sitting at his desk with a broad smile on his face. Bates just shook his head.

"You heard me . . ." and the screen went blank.

THE WOMAN

THE WOMAN

CHAPTER 16

Jake thought he heard a woman's voice again, but he could swear it wasn't Linda, and then he began to remember and imagine how it probably happened.

Another scene appeared, and there was Annette Montoya, widow of Carlos Montoya, a brilliant hedge fund operator who had made a fortune. She sat on a balcony of one of her many homes . . . this one on Sunset Key, a resort she co-owned, sitting in the Gulf, just west of Key West. She continued to chain smoke, as if it made a difference now, since she was suffering from Stage IV metastatic lung cancer, and sipped on a strawberry margarita. A motor boat, which she knew had come from Cuba, approached her dock.

A man dressed in dark clothing, along with someone who looked like a body builder and whom she assumed was his guard, stepped onto the dock, the boat being tied up by one of her servants. She did not know their names and realized that she never would, nor did she care to. They were simply a means to an end for her.

CHAPTER 17

She had grown up poor in Bahama Village and had few friends at Key West High School. Only one person had been kind to her . . . Martin Polanco . . . always speaking to her when he saw her. It was enough. She fell madly in love with him. He was handsome, tall, a baseball star, and class president. She worked and saved everything she could to scrape together the money to buy a second-hand prom gown. She had always been pretty, but had never had the money to be what was considered beautiful.

The days of her senior school year passed, and she ran into Martin one time after the other. For some reason, she knew this would finally be the day, but he never asked her, and then she heard those dreadful, hurtful girls talking behind her back as she stood by her locker. Martin had asked Terri Gibson. They were all screaming. The beautiful blonde-haired cheerleader, and her chief tormentor, was going with the boy she loved to the prom. She stood there shaking with emotion, tears streaming down her cheeks . . . her face hidden in her locker so no one could see her.

She had wiped her face and turned just as Martin approached, and she smiled and gazed at him, her heart beating in her chest, but he simply ignored her and walked past her and put his arms around Terri Gibson.

At that point in her life, a cold spot formed in her heart. Her passion changed to hatred . . . hatred for all those who had what she did not have . . . and she vowed she would do whatever was necessary to have them . . . and ultimately, she would have her revenge.

Her climb up the social ladder began with her marriage to a banker in Virginia. The divorce got her some money, not enough for everything she wanted, but enough to get her to the next level . . . the plastic surgery, the spas, the classes to become cultured. She did it all, and that led her to Carlos.

She had arrived. She had kept her vow. She had it all. And now, she would have her revenge.

THE PLAN

CHAPTER 18

The darkness had come back and then quickly was gone. Jake felt tethered in the air, the light and dark coming in a certain rhythm. Sounds, some familiar and some not... some far off and some close... and the movie playing in his mind went on, scene after scene...

Mike arrived at the airport in Key West on the Monday before the scheduled reunion in a private FSI jet, and Jake was there to meet him.

"Aren't you the corporate executive?" asked Jake, seeing Mike dressed in a sports coat, oxford cloth shirt, and khakis.

"Yeah, you look really... nice... too," said Mike, looking up and down at Jake's t-shirt, shorts, and slip-on Keds.

Jake held out his arms and said, "Welcome to paradise!" and then slapped Mike on the shoulder.

As they headed out of the airport, Hector, the jack of all trades, was acting as chauffer, using his car for the pickup.

"Hey, Hector, how are you doing?" said Mike as he held out his hand. Hector nodded and opened the door for him to get in. When Jake and Mike were seated,

Mike leaned over and whispered to Jake, "I see his personality hasn't changed."

Jake laughed and just nodded.

In route, they engaged in small talk about Charlotte, Linda, and where they were at in their respective lives. Jake was still happy for Mike, but there was a pang when he considered his own situation.

"I'm really glad you two are happy," said Jake, looking out the window, as the island scenes went past.

"Thanks. I appreciate it," said Mike, "and don't worry . . . everything is going to work out all right for you, too."

"Time will tell, buddy . . . time will tell."

They finally pulled up in front of the office and Hector exited the car, opening the door once again for Mike.

"Thanks, Hector," Mike said, again soliciting another nod, and he looked at Jake. "I seem to remember the last time I looked at this. Wasn't it just a pile of blown-up rubble?"

"Something like that," said Jake. "Come on, I'll show you around."

When Mike entered the door, Eva bounded out of her chair and hugged him, kissing him on the cheek.

"You can't believe how glad I am to see you two together again!" she gushed.

"Me, too," said Mike, "but you know, it's not permanent. We can't have too much of a good thing," he said laughing.

"Don't worry," said Jake, walking past him, "I'll send you packing as soon as I don't need you anymore."

Mike followed him into Jake's office.

"You always need me, Jake. You know that." Eva returned to her desk, laughing and clapping her hands.

"Just like old times," she said, looking at Hector, who simply shook his head, not sure of the entire thing. Mike had just sat down when he had to get back up again and shake Sam Walsh's hand as he came into Jake's office.

"How do you like the new digs?" Sam asked.

"Better than the FBI. I'll tell you that. Not a bad location either here in paradise, is it?"

"Not from what I've seen," said Sam, "although Mr. Sullivan tends to keep me locked up in that little room back there."

Jake laughed.

"All right, Sam, give him what we've got."

"Well," said Sam, "following up on what I've told you already, I've been tracking known assassins with a connection to Group 45, listening to every piece of chatter I can, looking for money transfers, deposits, anything . . . and checking all the known communications and all the informants we have. And I've come up with . . . absolutely nothing."

Mike looked at him and shook his head.

"Hell of a job," and then looked at Jake. "Now what?"

"What can I tell you, Mike?" said Jake. "My gut tells me it's the real deal."

"Then that's what we're going with," said Mike.

"Let's get everything ready."

CHAPTER 19

Jake and Mike had just strolled into the Pier House when Mike put out his hand to stop them.

"Is that who I think it is?" he said, as he pointed to Lester Kirkland, the former Attorney General.

Jake pulled Mike aside and talked in a low voice.

"He's the head of the Vice President's security team through a private company that's working with the Secret Service. The rumor is that he wasn't asked to join FSI, and he wasn't too happy about it. He took a job at a top security agency, and right away had two great successes . . . involved in shootouts where he stopped the assassination of a Saudi businessman in Riyadh and uncovered a plot against a CIA station chief in Jerusalem."

"Not bad," said Mike. "I wonder . . ." but he was cut off, as Lester Kirkland bounded toward them, hand now extended.

"Well, look who's here."

Jake took his hand first.

"Lester, good to see you. How've you been?"

"Great, great . . . how about you guys?" he said, now shaking Mike's hand.

"Same old game," said Mike, "just a new ball field."

"Speaking of that," said Jake, "how do you like your new quarterback? The Irish going to win it all this year?"

"Hey, I think Notre Dame has finally found the real deal. It's been a while."

"I didn't know you went to Notre Dame," said Mike.

"Yeah, I was going to be a priest until the Naval Academy came calling . . . and now, here I am. Sometimes I think I made the wrong decision."

"Don't we all?" said Mike. "Don't we all?"

CHAPTER 20

Annette Montoya arose from the patio and walked to the dock, extending her hand to the man with no name. She enjoyed it as he stared at her face and figure, as they always did, but she never let on that she enjoyed it, and her composure was one of cold indifference.

This man had come to her on another one of her trips to Key West, appearing out of the darkness. He had worked with her husband on certain monetary transactions to which she was not privy. He had known of her illness. In fact, he had known everything about her, especially her deep-seated hatred for Martin Polanco, and he had offered her a way to obtain her revenge.

It was a simple choice for her. The end she now faced was much simpler and less painful than the one she was expecting. She was not interested in politics and knew there would be someone to take his place. The coldness that had eaten at her for years made it easy, and now the time was finally here.

"Have a seat and a cold drink," she said, as she walked ahead of him, up the dock to the patio, knowing full well that his gaze was fixed on her undulating hips and the tightness of her shorts. We'll discuss final preparations."

They sat down and he began.

"You must listen very carefully. There can be no mistakes."

She put up her hand to stop him.

"You do know who you're talking to, don't you? I've only made one mistake in my life, and that's these," she said, holding up a lit cigarette. "You need not worry about me, Señor. I will do my part, and I will do it well. Just make sure what I need is available, as we discussed, and I will take care of the rest."

It felt good talking to him like that, and she knew she was ready. In fact, she was looking forward to it.

THE REUNION

CHAPTER 21

In the darkness that overtook the light again, Jake saw the headlights of newly washed and waxed vehicles as they pulled up to the Pier House valet.

Mike and Jake were both dressed in dark suits and they were walking the grounds. They passed the open doors to the Chart Room and the bartender looked up.
"Hey, Mr. Sullivan . . . how's it going?"
"Good Michael. How are you?"
"Living the dream, as always."
"Isn't it the truth?" asked Jake.
They then entered the main lobby and ran into Kirkland and one of his men. The man, who had a name tag stating he was James Foster, spoke to Kirkland.
"We checked everything again – any place where anything could be concealed or hidden. I'm going to do the men's and ladies' rooms again just to be sure."
"You know, I have a better idea," said Kirkland, "go out and check around the beachfront. I think if anything is coming, it's coming in by water. I'll take care of the bathrooms."
"Whatever you say, boss," said Foster, as he walked away.

"Still making those big decisions, I see," said Mike.

"Comes with the territory. You know that. This place is locked down tighter than a drum. We have the Coast Guard, patrolling the beach, we have a perimeter set up a block in each direction, we've had the dogs in and checked for explosives, we've done a scan for all virals and toxins, and we have all doors locked and guarded except for the main one coming in, and metal detectors are set up there. We've got rooftop snipers all along the V.P.'s route in addition to the Secret Service's own security, which basically doubles ours."

"Sounds like you've got everything set," said Mike.

"Did you boys ever think you might have been played on this one?" asked Kirkland.

"Always a possibility," said Jake.

CHAPTER 22

As they were moving back outside and were walking through the lush greenery that bordered the path to the beach area, Sam Walsh called in again.

"Go ahead, Sam, you're on speaker," said Jake.

"I've gone over everything. I've gone over the list of the attendees one more time. There are no additions that don't pass muster. I can't find anything of interest. All names check with graduates of the class. Addresses are all accurate. We've checked people who've come to Key West and where they're staying . . . done facial recognition scans . . . everybody seems to be who they say they are. There's nobody out of place."

"Maybe Kirkland's right," said Jake. "Maybe we were played."

"I'm still going with your gut," said Mike. "The bad guy's here. We just have to find him."

CHAPTER 23

Right before the reunion starting time, a black Bentley pulled up to the Pier House. The car and its occupant were well-known to the valet.

"Good evening, Mrs. Montoya. Here for the reunion, I take it?"

"Well, yes, Steven . . . I am," she said, having rolled down the back window. "It's a beautiful night, don't you think?"

"And I hope you're going to have a beautiful time, ma'am."

"Why, thank you Steven."

"Here . . . let me help you out. You can have your usual parking spot. It hasn't been taken yet," he said to the driver.

Annette Montoya worked her way out of the back seat, taking the hand of Steven, and she could not help but notice that he gave her the once-over. She was tan and her hair was perfect, as was her makeup. Her white gown clung to her form, and she batted her eyes and smiled at Steven, still knowing she could turn heads.

She entered the Pier House and passed her purse through the metal detector, and the machine monitor smiled, knowing that her dress was obviously not hiding anything, and she passed through without incident.

She walked out into the lush greenery that was the Pier House landscape and made her way toward the beach and took a seat at the bar, happy to have found her favorite bartenders, Janine and her sister Merri, were handling the festivities.

"Welcome, Mrs. Montoya," said Janine. "The usual?"

"Please," she said, and sat back to wait for her strawberry margarita.

Just then, a heavyset woman with blonde hair approached her. The name tag said she was Lucy Cantor.

"Welcome to the reunion. How are you?"

"None of your business, you little troll," thought the widow, but she smiled and said, "I'm fine, Lucy," punctuating the name. "Now, please excuse me. I must use the little girl's room," and she turned and walked off.

CHAPTER 24

Annette went to the restroom and entered the second stall, as she had been directed. There, she put down the toilet seat and stepped up on top and moved the second ceiling tile out of place, balancing herself with her hand against the wall. She reached around, but there was nothing there. She tried again, moving her fingers and hit something metallic. She stretched and grasped the barrel of a .38 revolver. She replaced everything, flushed the toilet, and came out and washed her hands and put the .38 into her purse. She looked at the mirror, posed, smiled, and raised the drink she had carried in and set on the sink in front of her.

"To a perfect night, darling," and then she returned to the reunion.

CHAPTER 25

Annette couldn't help but notice, and loved the fact, that all eyes were on her as she small-talked with some of her classmates while they all were waiting for the great man to arrive. So many didn't recognize her, and why should they? She had reinvented herself and become more than they would ever be, and after tonight, there was no doubt in her mind that she would be remembered forever by all of them.

It was while she was engaged in such conversation that a great deal of activity erupted on the path leading to the beach. A contingent of Secret Service and other men entered the beach area in their nondescript black suits and no-nonsense looks. And then he was among them . . . Martin Polanco . . . Vice President of the United States.

CHAPTER 26

"*Still tall, dark, and handsome,*" thought the widow, as she moved toward him as he posed for photographers. And then suddenly a chubby blonde, in a too tight-fitting dress with a pasty face that indicated the consumption of too much alcohol, was standing beside him.

"*Ah, how perfect,*" thought the widow, looking at the name tag that she sported, "*the cheerleader and her hero,*" as she recognized Terri Gibson. She approached them and held out her hand.

"Mr. Vice President . . ." and she realized he could not place her . . . he didn't recognize her. She spoke softly, "You don't remember me, do you, Martin? I was Annette Thompson."

The cow beside him gasped, and Martin was taken aback.

"Annette," he stammered, looking at her from top to bottom, "so good to see you," and he took her hand in his.

"Can I please get an autograph?" she cooed, removing her hand and opening her purse.

"Of course," said Polanco.

But no pen came out of the purse . . . only the .38 . . . and even before the nearest agent could yell, "Gun!" he put two shots into Martin Polanco's heart and one in the cheerleader's eye as she whispered, "You picked the wrong date, Martin."

Then she turned toward the Secret Service agent bearing down on her and aimed the gun, as he fired two shots in her direction. She slumped to the floor, as blood erupted from her chest, soaking the beautiful white gown and the sand beneath her, and a smile formed on her face as she breathed her last.

Jake, Mike, and Kirkland rushed to the scene. They and the Secret Service sealed off the area, making sure no one left. It was clear Polanco was dead, as well as another female and the shooter. Mike looked at Jake.

"I guess I was wrong about the bad guy," he said. "We should have been looking for a bad woman. We are in a true shit storm, my friend."

"You think?" asked Jake, shaking his head, as he took in the scene around him.

THE FALLOUT

CHAPTER 27

A man was on an encrypted phone, sitting on the veranda of an isolated estate along the north shore of Cuba.

"Is everything in place as we planned?"

"Yes. The decision has already been made, just as we expected. The shooting has been written off as the desperate act of a dying woman consumed by jealousy and hatred. Your plan worked perfectly. You picked the perfect person."

"Yes . . . and even more importantly, Jason Adams will be the next Vice President. You're sure about the votes in the House and the Senate?"

"Absolutely. He is well respected, and he and his technological empire will soon be ours."

"I will follow through with everything else and I will be in touch."

The man stood up, took a cigar from a humidor, and went through a ritual in lighting it. He looked out over the sea, very satisfied . . . very satisfied, indeed.

CHAPTER 28

Months went by. The debacle in Key West was being investigated by congressional committees, the Justice Department, the FBI, and, internally, at FSI. The questions centered around how she was able to have the gun after going through the metal detector, and the Secret Service, along with Kirkland's team and along with FSI, were being looked at, and no one could exclude the possibility that someone in their organization was involved.

Hearings were scheduled immediately, and Jake and everyone else involved took their turn testifying before Congress as to what they had done, what they observed, and anyone they might suspect. The August recess was cancelled and the hearings droned on, and Jake took his turn and testified, but did not reveal what he already knew . . . that Group 45 was involved, that it had been their plan, and that the only purpose in carrying out the plot was to ensure that one of them would be the new Vice President, and his focus was not on the assassination, but on Jason Adams.

THE NEW VICE PRESIDENT

CHAPTER 29

Jake could feel the agitation building in his system. It wasn't really a movement, but the shifts between lightness and dark were upsetting him, and he could feel his body react as he thought back to his frustration.

It was late. Jake was sitting on the couch, staring at a football game he wasn't even watching, drinking a Diet Coke, and lost in thought. It was too clean . . . the dots all connecting in a straight line. He didn't believe for a second that Annette Montoya acted alone in assassinating Vice President Martin Polanco. She was a pawn who had been used by Group 45 and, if that was true, for what end? The answer to Jake was obvious . . . to get someone as close as possible to the seat of power in United States government . . . a new Vice President under their thumb . . . a heartbeat away from the Presidency.

The problem was, after digging as deep as he could, he could find nothing even remotely sinister in the dossier he compiled on Jason Adams, the man President Turner had selected to be his new Vice President.

A technical genius, a graduate of MIT, and an ancestry that went the whole way back to John Adams,

he had made great strides in fields that helped many people. . . medical, biological, and in communications. He gave a great deal of his fortune away to charity.

He seemed to be apolitical, not really affiliated with any party, but basing his considerations on common sense and what was best for the country and its people... a political anachronism in this day and age.

Jake threw the file he had been reading on the coffee table in front of him and got up and walked around.

"Maybe I'm wrong. Maybe she was some person who harbored such animosity that she would kill in such a public fashion, but it was those visits . . . those visits from the boat that didn't fit in to everyone's current theory. Who was she meeting with and why? And why had she gone against the prevailing system that whenever a non-registered boat arrived, it was checked in and the names of all on board, as well as their purpose, was noted in a log. But she had called in advance the three times that those in the boat had come to see her, and asked that they be afforded privacy and that she would explain at a later date . . . and, as always, her wishes had been complied with."

"No," said Jake, shaking his head, "there's something wrong here, and it's tied to Group 45 and their leader . . . their leader in Cuba, ninety miles away by boat."

He looked at the clock on the wall. It was only 8:30. He took out his cell phone and made the call.

"Jason, this is Jake Sullivan. I need to see the President."

"Tonight?" barked Bates in reply.

"Don't get all excited, Jason. I was thinking about flying up tomorrow and meeting with him at a time that was convenient."

"You know his schedule," said Bates, "no time is convenient."

"Look, Jason, it's important. Fit me in, will you?"

"Yeah, yeah," said Bates. "Let me know when you touch down. I'll get you in, but what's this about?"

"It's private, Jason. If you don't mind, it's something I need to discuss only with the President."

"Why is it when you say things like that I know there is a disaster looming somewhere?"

"Nothing like that, Jason. Don't worry. It's just a hunch."

"As if I haven't heard that before," and the phone went dead as Jason hung up.

Jake looked at the phone and managed a smile and thought to himself, *"At least some things never change."*

CHAPTER 30

As usual, Bates was more bark than bite and Jake got a call early in the morning that the corporate jet was fueled and waiting for him at the airport in Key West.

Since coming to the island, Jake had afforded himself one luxury, since he had been able to find almost an exact replica of the 2006 BMW Z4 that had been destroyed on his first stay on the island. With the top down, it was a beautiful morning drive, and Jake decided to take the scenic route, taking Whitehead to Eaton, he turned right onto Duval, reveling in the quiet of the early morning as the sidewalks were hosed off and cleaned from the festivities of the night before. Turning onto South at the Southern Most Point, he drove to White and glanced out at the rising sun in the Atlantic as he headed on Atlantic Boulevard to South Roosevelt and the Key West International Airport.

The flight itself was uneventful, and he played over the various scenarios of Polanco's death in his mind, but he couldn't shake the feeling that Group 45 was somehow involved. A little under two and a half hours and he was on the ground at Ronald Reagan Washington National Airport, an FSI car waiting for him.

Fletcher Security and Investigations, leased with intent to buy, the entire office building located at 2031 M

Street on the edge of Georgetown, and Jake spent his time en route looking out the backseat window as the monuments and the sights of D.C. flashed by.

He had called Bates, and he was there waiting for him in the lobby when Jake entered.

"Look, Jake, I got you a half hour. He's really pressed today, so in and out, all right?"

Jake stopped walking, which made Bates do the same, and they looked at each other.

"You do know, Jason, that he isn't President any longer?"

Bates expression never changed. He just turned and started walking again.

"I know, I know . . . but his time is still important."

"All right, Jason, all right . . . I promise . . . no more than a half hour."

"Good," said Bates as he punched in the top floor on the elevator and they headed up.

As Jake was ushered into Fletcher's office, he couldn't help but notice that the office reflected the man – nothing ostentatious, but solid, suitably decorated with only a few photographs and pieces of memorabilia indicating that the white-haired man at the large wooden desk was the former President of the United States.

He sprung out of his seat as Jake entered and walked around the desk and held out his hand.

"Jake, it's been too long. Good to see you!" shaking his hand and putting his other hand on Jake's shoulder, as he had done so many times before. "Please, sit. So what's going on that necessitated this face-to-face meeting?"

"Sorry, Mr. President," said Jake, " but I have one of those itches I just can't seem to scratch."
Fletcher had sat down and tented his hands on the desk in front of him and leaned back, his hands moving toward his face.

"I see, I see," he mused, looking out one of the large windows that gave a beautiful view of the nation's capital. "Well, Jake," he said, slamming his palms on the desk, "let's hear it. Your itches haven't been too wrong in the past, if I remember correctly."

"I know, sir, but this one just might be," and he began to tell his suspicions about the assassination of Vice President Martin Polanco.

Fletcher listened intently the whole way through the story and had gotten up and walked around his office, staring out the window occasionally, never asking a question, but listening to every word that Jake said.

"And that's it, Mr. President. That's the itch I can't scratch."

Fletcher nodded his head and sat down.

"I can understand, Jake. The boat thing is something we need to look into, but I have some information that might put your mind at ease."

Jake looked at him quizzically as Fletcher continued.

"I'm afraid I used my power in this one, Jake. I pulled a few strings. I'm sure you know that Jason went to MIT, correct?"

"That's what my research showed, Mr. President."

"Right, right . . . well, I don't know how much you've dealt with his genealogy, but his grandfather was an old Yale man, and actually, Jonathan Adams and I were quite close friends and I got to know the family – Jason's father, Robert, and Jason himself. I hope this eases your worry, Jake, but I'm the one who convinced President Turner to pick Jason for the VP slot. He's smart, he's a patriot, and I think his technological skills are something that we can use in this changing world of ours, so, after his father indicated he would be interested, I pushed for him. It's as simple as that, and, even though I'm a former President, sometimes we still get what we ask for."

Jake was both relieved and upset.

"Were there any other outside sources pushing for his nomination, Mr. President?"

"Sure, some, but I made the decision, Jake. Just me. His name never came up until I brought it up . . . and actually, there were quite a few people who didn't want to jump on the bandwagon with me on this one. They thought we should give it to someone who had been loyal to the party and were concerned about how Jason might fare should he decide to run for President in the future. I sort of backhanded those concerns, Jake. I had made up my mind that this young man was good for the country, and it was my decision."

"I see," said Jake.

"I'll tell you what," said Fletcher, rising and looking at the watch on his wrist, "I have another meeting to attend to, but I'll look into this boat thing personally and get some people on it, and if I find anything, you'll be the first to know, and we'll reconsider this whole idea. Understand, I'm not happy it's the case, but I think the death of poor Martin Polanco was simply the act of a spiteful, deranged woman who had nothing to lose, facing a long and painful death, as she was. I've talked to a couple of psychiatrists about this whole thing. They all came to the same conclusion – that this reunion event and her disease was what triggered the whole thing. It gave her the perfect chance to strike back at those she had felt belittled her when she was young, and now that she had become what she had wanted, she couldn't enjoy it because of her disease. They said it was the perfect storm, and I guess they were right."

Jake stood up as Fletcher extended his hand, coming around the desk.

"Well, that settles it, Mr. President. Thank you very much. I'm relieved to hear that there's no involvement by the bad guys in this one."

"I don't think so, Jake," said Fletcher, laughing. "I think I'm still on the side of the angels."

"I wasn't questioning that, Mr. President."

"I know, I know," said Fletcher, laughing and slapping him on the back, "but don't stop listening to your gut. It's served you and this country very well so far. By the way, before you leave, any new leads on who the new leader of this despicable group might be?"

"Not yet, sir. Everybody's still working on it."

Fletcher turned, his hand still on his back, ushering him toward the door. Jake smiled to himself. President Fletcher was one of those amazing people that could make you feel wanted, even when he was pushing you out.

"You seeing Mike while you're in town?"

"As a matter of fact, I am. He and Charlotte Kosior and I are having dinner tonight."

"Wonderful! Wonderful!" said Fletcher. "You all have a great time, and keep me posted on anything else that's going on."

"I will, sir, and thank you for your time."

Fletcher looked over at Bates as he stood in the doorway.

"All right, Jason, let's get the next group in here."

"Yes, Mr. President," said Bates, and gave a sideways glance at Jake.

"What?" said Jake.

Bates looked at his watch.

"Hey, don't blame me. He did all the talking," said Jake, smiling, as he left the suite of offices and headed for the elevator. As he rode it down two floors to the office he kept in the Washington, D.C., headquarters, his mind was focused on two things that former President Jordan Fletcher had said . . . "*Some*" people had pushed for Adams, and "*Keep listening to your gut.*" He was, and it was telling him that there was something . . . something out of place . . . but for the life of him, given what he had just heard, Jake couldn't figure out what it was.

CHAPTER 31

Jake could see the inside of the office and hear the noise of the other offices around him as he thought back.

Mike was out at another congressional hearing and, as they had planned when Jake had called him about his trip, they had agreed they would meet at the office later, and then meet Charlie at Mac's.

The thought of Mac's homemade chili made him realize he hadn't eaten and how hungry he was, and he ordered a Caesar salad from the office cafeteria to hold him over.

His office in Key West was connected to his office in FSI headquarters in Washington and he did a video conference with Eva so he could be updated on everything that she had received so far that day. Things were quiet, and he dealt with the normal day-to-day things by giving her instructions. They had worked so long together that she knew what he was going to say before he said it, and he smiled to himself realizing that Eva could probably take care of everything herself, even though she deferred to him and let him think that he was the boss.

When they had finished he checked the other national and international transmissions that had come into the D.C. office to all its various parts and sent out instructions to the various agencies as to what they should be doing and then ran a deep inquiry into Jonathan and Robert Adams . . . and came up with nothing. By that evening, he had completed all of his tasks and made up his mind that he was no longer going to concentrate on the new Vice President. He had come to the conclusion that he had difficulty accepting that his gut had been wrong.

"*It's my ego*," he thought. Everyone telling him about his legendary ability to figure things out based on his intuition and his skill at reading the facts that no one else seemed to see. "*What a bunch of horse shit*," he thought, as he packed everything up for the day and took the elevator down one floor to Mike's office, hoping he would be in.

His hopes were rewarded. As he got off the elevator and walked down the hall and made a left to the corner office, the door was open. He tapped at it once and went in. Mike looked up from his desk, where he was huddled over a pile of papers.

"Burning the midnight oil, I see. About time."

"Ah, look," said Mike, "the prodigal beach bum has returned."

Jake had worn khaki slacks, a blue button-down oxford cloth shirt, and a navy blazer to his meeting with President Fletcher, as Mike stood up and looked down at his feet.

"Wow! Not even flip-flops!"

"Hey, come on. He *was* the President of the United States. I have to give him some respect."

"You never cease to amaze me," said Mike, sitting down.

"Come on. Pack it in and let's go. I'm hungry."

"Chile, huh?" asked Mike, as he closed a file and smiled at Jake.

"Absolutely. Charlie good to go?"

"Yeah, I just talked to her. She's on her way. She'll save us a booth."

"Great. I can't remember how long it's been since you and I ate at Mac's."

"Don't worry. Nothing's changed. Mac's as irascible as ever."

"That's okay," said Jake, as they headed out the door, "that's the way I like him."

CHAPTER 32

The darkness passed and Jake smiled to himself as he thought of Mac.

Charlie waved at them as they entered the restaurant portion of the bar and she stood up as they approached and hugged Mike and kissed him and then hugged Jake and gave him a peck on the cheek.
"It's good to see you," said Charlie.
"Good to see you, young lady. I hope this jerk isn't giving you too much trouble."
"Nothing I can't handle," said Charlie, as she smiled at Mike and they took their seats. Charlie reached over and put her hand on top of Jake's on the table. "Anything changed?"
"Afraid not."
"I'm sorry, Jake," she said, true concern in her eyes.
"It's one of those things that just has to play itself out."
"The girls okay?"
"Yeah. We talk pretty regularly. They're doing fine."
Just then, a voice boomed out behind them.

"I don't know what you three are talking about, but it better be my chili!"

Jake didn't even have to turn around. He was up out of his chair with his hand out as Mac approached. Mac pushed his hand away and put him in a bear hug.

"How you doing young man? It's been a while."

"Too long, Mac," said Jake, "too long."

And then he shook Mike, who had also stood, by the shoulder.

"And what about this one? Can you imagine, ending up with such a beautiful young lady?"

"I know," said Jake, "hard to believe, isn't it?"

"How are you, my dear?" said Mac, bowing toward Charlie.

"I'm fine, Mac. Good to see you."

Jake patted Mac on the belly.

"Looks like prosperity suits you."

Mac looked around at the bar and restaurant, smiling. "Yeah, things are going pretty well. You know, I do have customers who drink more than Diet Coke."

"I do know that," said Jake, "I used to be one of them, if I recall."

"Well, you're smarter than the rest of us, son."

"If you're done insulting me," said Mike, "would you mind sending over a waitress so we can order some of that slop that you designate as your world famous chili?"

Mac squinted at him and then looked up at the ceiling, his hand brushing over his chin.

"You know, I'm pretty sure we only have two bowls left," he said, and then again slapped Mike on the shoulder. "Your order has been in. It'll be here soon, and for this joyous celebration, it's on the house."

"No Mac, don't do that," said Jake.

"My bar, my rules," said Mac. "Enjoy!" and he turned around, yelling at one of the staff, "Get this table cleaned up! We have people waiting!"

"Well," said Jake, "you were right . . . irascible as ever!"

"Isn't that the truth," said Mike, as Charlie laughed.

The rest of the evening was spent eating the world's best chili, talking about Charlie's new job at the Smithsonian, Jake's daughters, their prior adventures in Montana, and anything else that could make them smile and laugh. The street lights were just coming on as they exited and said their goodbyes.

Mac had called Jake a cab before they left and it was waiting for him at the curb.

"All right, you two. Take care of each other. Keep your eyes and ears open, Mike. We still have to find this guy."

"Don't worry, Jake, we will."

"I have no doubt," said Jake as he opened the door and took a seat in the cab, rolled down the window, and said, "Charlie, get him to bring you down to Key West and I'll take you on the Duval Crawl."

"This from a man who drinks Diet Coke," said Mike.

With that, Jake smiled, the window went up, and he was gone.

Charlie put her arm inside Mike's as they walked down the street.

"How's he really doing?"

"This thing with Linda is killing him, that I know, but there's something else nagging at him."

"What do you mean?"

"Jake's my best friend. I know him as well as I know myself. He has one of those feelings of his, but I think he's looking at a riddle he can't solve."

"Can you help him?" asked Charlie.

"I hope so. We'll see," and they continued walking down the sidewalk on a warm late summer evening in Washington, D.C.

CHAPTER 33

Jake arrived back in Key West at approximately 11:00 P.M. that night, showered, checked anything that had come into the office after he spoke with Eva, took care of a few items, and then planned to go up to the apartment and get a good night's sleep.

The nagging was still there, but it was subsiding, and that's when Jake heard noise outside his office and Sam Walsh knocked on his door jam and everything began to change.

THE CLUE

CHAPTER 34

Jake had floated through space when he thought about the plane ride home, and he was calm and still, but then there was light and a sense of urgency as he recalled what happened next and how it changed everything.

"Jake, do you know anything about Parrotheads?"

"Sure, they're fans of Jimmy Buffett. They have clubs all over the country. Why?"

"I don't know. It might not be anything, but during the last month or so there have been five registrations with the Virtual Parrothead Club, a club you can join online . . . one each from Sicily, Mexico, the Ukraine, the Balkans, and Shanghai."

"Yeah, it's a worldwide thing, Sam. What's the issue?"

"Think what those places represent."

Jake stood up.

"Those are the home bases for the people we think are in the Group 45 leadership circle . . . and?"

"The registrations for all were aliases that we know those folks have used before. And one more thing," said Sam. "Right before they did it, I picked up a piece of chatter that didn't seem to make any sense. It appeared to be in Spanish, but it was hard to translate into something that made any sense in English, but the best I could do was 'ruler' or 'chief' . . . but the four letters that kept appearing . . . I just can't seem to break them down into any words that make any sense."

"What are the four letters?" asked Jake.

"As best I can make out, MOTM."

Jake sat back in his chair and smiled, and then sat upright.

"What is it, Jake? What have you got?" asked Sam.

"Let me tell you a little about the Parrotheads," he said. "Like I told you, they're followers of Jimmy Buffett, and there are clubs all around the United States, and all around the world, for that matter. Mostly, they go to Buffett concerts, they do charitable works, and, of course, they party . . . in point of fact, their motto is 'Party With A Purpose' . . . and they do. Go to any event that involves Buffett and you'll see bankers wearing grass skirts and coconut bras, pickup trucks filled with sand making their own beaches, blenders whirling in the back of soccer moms' cars . . . it's a big party. But every year, the Parrotheads get together for one national blowout. For a while it was held in New Orleans, but for the last twenty or so years, it's been held in Key West. You know what it's called?"

"Obviously not," said Sam.

"Meeting Of The Minds."

"Meeting Of The Minds?" asked Sam. "What in the world does that . . . holy shit!"

"Yeah . . . holy shit is right . . . Meeting Of The Minds, which is usually shortened to MOTM."

THE MEETING OF THE MINDS

CHAPTER 35

"So what happens at this Meeting Of The Minds thing?" asked Walsh.

"Like I said, there are Parrothead clubs all over the country and the world, and, their members, those that can, come every year to Key West for an annual get together. Do you listen to Jimmy Buffett?"

"Occasionally."

"You ever been to one of his concerts?"

"No."

"Well, you should. It is something to behold. People from all walks of life getting together, throwing off their daily problems and inhibitions, drinking too much, laughing too hard, and listening intently to the music played by the man on the stage. Buffett is the originator of a type of music that has come to be called Trop Rock. The songs all tend to deal with tropical places – the beach, palm trees, rum, and Buffett, himself. There's an organization that promotes the genre called the Trop Rock Music Association and they have an awards show, which is the Friday night of the Parrothead Convention, MOTM. It usually runs from Thursday through Saturday, although there are events that precede it and run on after it, but that's the basic time frame, and on Friday night of the convention is when the awards are given and the performers take the stage and it's a huge concert. Usually a lot of the members of the Coral Reefers Band, Jimmy Buffett's back-up crew, come and Buffett, himself, has been known to come on occasion, and play for his fans . . . so it's a long weekend party. But, as I told you, underneath the party, there are charitable works going on and business being conducted by the organizations and various Parrothead clubs involved. Hence, the nickname 'Party With A Purpose'. You have a good time, but you benefit others while you do it."

"Sounds like a good event."

"I've been to a couple. It's a great event. I've met a lot of good people. A lot of great musicians."

Walsh looked at him quizzically.

"When I was down here before, I ironed out some security issues, got to know some people, and you know how that goes."

Walsh nodded.

"Understood. So what do you think the play is here by Group 45, if there is one?"

"Given all that goes on, it'd be a heck of a place to conduct a meeting. Give a bad guy a floral shirt and a lei . . . he could fit right in."

"You think that's what they're doing?"

"Think about it. We're in Key West."

Walsh looked up at him and nodded slowly.

"Right under our noses . . . right under *your* nose."

"Exactly. This guy wants to get back at me for what I've done to him, and being elected the leader of

Group 45 in Key West where I'm on the job . . . there's nothing he'd like better."

"So where do we go from here?"

"Already taking care of it. Get some sleep. We're going to be on a conference call first thing in the morning with Fletcher and Mike and everybody else. We're going to cook up a little surprise of our own for our visiting 'Parrothead' friends."

CHAPTER 36

"All right, Sullivan," said Bates, who Jake could hear but not see on the screen. "Everyone's here, as you requested. What's going on?"

"Mr. President, Mike, everyone . . . Mr. Walsh has heard some new chatter. I'm going to let him explain what he's found out and what we think it means, and then we want to see how everyone thinks we should handle it. Go ahead, Sam."

Walsh went over the chatter he had heard, the explanations he had gotten from Jake and what it might mean, and the conclusion it had led to . . . that all of the section leaders of Group 45 were coming to Key West under cover of Meeting Of The Minds to hold a meeting to elect their leader.

Mike laughed and shook his head.

"You've got to give the guy credit, Jake! If he wants you to look badly as much as we think he does, this is a hell of a way to do it."

"My thoughts exactly," said Jake.

"Seems a little far-fetched though, doesn't it?" asked Fletcher. "I mean, they could certainly have a more secretive venue to carry out this meeting."

"Yes," said Jake, "but don't forget, sir, if Antonio Ortiz is who we think he is, the defacto leader of Group 45 who wants a meeting to legitimize himself, this is close to home for him. He's asserting his leadership. He's making everybody come to him . . . to pay homage . . . and fealty to him. His ego demands that. And his ego also demands that he does it in a way that makes me look like a fool. If you look at it from that perspective, it's perfect cover."

"All right," said Fletcher, "let's say I buy it . . . what do we do about it?"

"First of all, I'd like Mike to come down again and work with me on this."

"That's no problem," said Fletcher.

"Then we set up undercover operatives at Casa Marina, the host hotel for the convention, and elsewhere in Key West . . . the airport . . . everywhere. We invite the convention planners down here, explain to them what we think is going on, assure them that their people are safe, and then wait."

"One thing bothers me," said Fletcher. "As Mr. Walsh describes things, you're going to have about three thousand people in harm's way."

"That's why we do it all through surveillance," said Jake. "We watch the comings and goings. If they're going to have a meeting here, it's going to be in secret. There'll be some room rented in the Casa by one of the five in attendance and our undercover operatives will move on that room and that room only, once we know they're there."

"You think we can contain it?" asked Fletcher.

"If I didn't, I wouldn't suggest it, sir. I wouldn't put those people's lives at risk. That's why I'm going to stay off-site, and so is Mike. The people we use are going to have to be non-descript and off Group 45's radar. They have to be able to blend in, and we have to coordinate this thing . . . tightly . . . 24/7."

Fletcher looked around the room.

"Well, ladies and gentlemen . . . what do you think?"

Mike spoke up.

"Sir, I think it's plausible and probable, and we don't have anything else to go on. If we can pull this off, this can be the crushing blow to this organization that we've been looking for."

There were nods around the room.

"All right, Jake, you're on."

"I'll be there tonight, Jake," said Mike.

"We'll start working our end," said Fletcher. "We'll get the names and backgrounds together, get the false identities set up, and send everything to you for review. Once everything's agreed upon, we'll put it in place."

"This thing begins on November 1st. We're in the last weeks of September. We have a month. Let's give the planning phase two weeks and start implementing operation after that, just in case we have any early arrivals."

"Done," said Fletcher. "That's our schedule. All right everybody . . . let's get to it. Jake, I want up-to-the-minute reports on this. This can't go sideways on us. There are too many people involved."

"There will be no civilian involvement, Mr. President . . . you have my word."

"Good enough for me."

And with that, the transmission ended.

"All right," said Jake, "let's get to work."

CHAPTER 37

Just as Jake was finishing up his video conference and giving instructions to Walsh on how to proceed, a phone call was made and rerouted through multiple cell towers around the world from Washington to Miami and finally to an estate on the remote northern shore of Cuba.

"Plans have been changed, I'm afraid."

"What do you mean?"

"The meeting scheduled in Key West has been compromised."

The voice in Cuba became angry.

"How? Why? What happened?"

"You can thank your fried, Jake Sullivan."

"Again! He interferes again!"

"Calm down," came the rerouted voice. "Things have been taken care of and all is well. The meeting in Key West will continue as scheduled, but with stand-ins for the other participants. The real meeting will still be held, but it will be at your estate, and you will receive the necessary pledges of loyalty, and you will become the face of Group 45. Then we will bring you to Key West."

"I don't understand," replied the voice from Cuba.

"A decision has been made to eliminate our major problem. The meeting in Key West will be a trap, and you will be the bait."

The man who would become Leader smiled to himself.

"Sullivan . . . finally. Yes, his time has come."

"Yes, he is too curious about Mr. Adams and he will not let go. We thought you would like to participate."

"You have no idea. It will be my honor."

"Excellent. We will be in touch to make the necessary arrangements."

Then the line went dead.

The man poured a margarita from an ice-filled pitcher on a side cart and walked to the railing, looked out over the water, and smiled.

"I told you that night I was going to come for you . . . and now I am," and then he lifted the glass in a toast to his unseen enemy.

CHAPTER 38

The movie in his head began again as he thought about Mike's arrival and what came next.

Mike arrived in Key West later that evening, and Jake met him at the airport. Looking over Mike's attire – a polo shirt, shorts, and sandals – he smiled.

"Well, I'm glad to see you're getting into the spirit of the island."

"Hey, I can be just as loose and breezy as the next guy, you know."

"I don't think I'd quite describe you as 'loose and breezy', Mike, but I'm glad you're here."

They both smiled and shook hands and walked to where Jake had parked his BMW.

"So what do you think of this whole, whatever it's called, 'Meeting Of The Minds' thing? You think these guys are really doing this?"

"Walsh thinks so, and I trust him. If you think about it, it's a pretty good cover."

"Yeah, I know, and the part about making you look bad makes sense, too. I have to tell you, I was coming down whether you asked for me or not . . . 'cause

I'm probably the only person who can save you from yourself and making yourself look bad."

Jake looked over at Mike and smiled as they headed down Roosevelt Boulevard.

"And don't think I don't appreciate it."

"I've got to admit, this is more like us, you know, Jake? Instead of sitting in an office in Washington, D.C., here I am in Key West chasing bad guys. I think the whole thing is going to make for a great vacation."

"You know, only you would think that confronting the guys that run one of the most ruthless organizations the world has ever seen, hiding in the midst of three thousand Parrotheads, constitutes a vacation."

Mike looked over at Jake.

"What else would you call it?" as he started to fiddle with the radio. "Might as well get in the spirit. This thing play any Jimmy Buffett?"

And they headed to Jake's apartment in Old Town.

THE PARROTHEADS

CHAPTER 39

Jake and Mike spent the next few weeks coordinating all the undercover operatives that came into Key West at various times and by various means. No one came near the office on Whitehead, but were met at various locations off island or at resorts. All communications were encrypted, and everything was on a need-to-know basis.

They were in the office going over a list of contacts they had to make within the community.

"What about the management team at the Casa Marina?" asked Mike, looking down at the list.

"Fletcher and I agree we have to keep them in the dark," said Jake. "Fletcher got us a Presidential Warrant for this operation, so we have powers of arrest and detention, even though we're private. Given that Group 45 decided to hold their meeting at the Casa Marina, it could mean they have somebody on the inside, and that's the last person we want to tip off. Fletcher has a buddy high up with Waldorf-Astoria and is coordinating with him."

"Good point," said Mike. Looking at another list, he said, "So, our undercovers there are going to be primarily convention attendees?"

"Yeah, I confirmed a meeting with the leaders of the Parrot Head organization after I got their tacit approval to have some undercover operatives be given convention credentials. The leadership is coming in tomorrow so they can get a final review of what's going on."

"You're not worried about these guys, then?" asked Mike.

"No. I've dealt with all of them in the past. Like I said, I did a couple of security things the last time I was living down here. They're just ordinary folks working for a good organization."

"I've got to admit," said Mike, "I don't get this whole Parrothead thing. I mean, I listen to Buffett occasionally and I like his music, but . . . this is wild."

"Look at it this way, it just gives some ordinary folks who work all types of jobs and live normal lives who maybe spend their winters in North Dakota, a chance to be in the tropics and just have fun . . . while at the same time doing some good charitable work. They get to live that laid-back lifestyle that Buffett sings about, even if only briefly. There's no harm to it. It's fun. I think it's great."

Mike looked at him, digesting what he was telling him.

"So how'd you get involved in this? How'd you become a Parrothead?"

Jake laughed.

"A long time ago, I had a friend who told me about Jimmy Buffett, who I had heard of but never gotten too involved with, and I knew the one song, *Margaritaville*, and that was basically it. And he told me about the concerts and how much fun they were and we should go to one. So, finally, after him going after me again and again, I agreed. But before we went, he gave me a CD called 'Songs You Know By Heart' – basically a compilation of Buffett's greatest hits. Some of those songs really stuck with me, and then we went to the concert and I saw all the people having such a good time, listening to the music, watching Buffett perform . . . I mean, the man's a great performer . . . and that was it. We just kept going back. Linda and I really liked it, and so did the girls."

Mike shook his head.

"I don't know, Jake. I'm not sure I get it."

"Okay, but don't knock it if you haven't tried it, buddy. Maybe I'll take you to a concert. We'll get you to become a Parrothead."

Mike went back to reading the files in front of him, shaking his head sideways.

"Highly doubtful . . . but I'll give it a shot," he said, looking up and smiling.

"All right. Let's see who else we have to vet," and they both went back to the paperwork.

CHAPTER 40

The final thing Jake and Mike did during the month of September was meet with the leaders of Parrotheads In Paradise, the national organization responsible for the holding of the Meeting Of The Minds convention in Key West. Jake had known the Head of Conventions, Andrew Talbert, due to past security issues he had been consulted on when previously in Key West.

However, given the brief outline of the meeting that Jake had provided, Talbert had requested that the entire Board attend a meeting at a site in the Middle Keys.

Jake and Mike entered a home that FSI had rented, through a dummy corporation, and found six meeting participants waiting for them.

"Mike, allow me to introduce Andrew Talbert, the Head of Conventions for Parrotheads In Paradise."

Mike shook Talbert's extended hand, as did Jake.

"Andrew, how've you been?"

"Fine, Jake, until I got the call from you. Now I'm a little bit concerned. That's why I asked the whole Board to be here. Let me introduce everybody. This is our President, Kathy Pfister, Vice President Rick Fyffe, Secretary David Cohen, Director of Finance Charlene Schultheis, and Director of Membership Sue Kermis."

There were brief hellos and nods around the room, and then Jake and Mike took their seats at the table, and Andrew began his questioning.

"I've got to tell you, Jake, you telling me that there could be a 'situation' at this year's event without being able to give me details is quite disconcerting to me and the rest of the folks here. You do realize we have three thousand people we owe a responsibility to?"

Jake put up his hand.

"Andrew, I know and I understand. We are concerned that a meeting could take place at this event. We believe that meeting will be held in one of the designated meeting rooms at the Casa and that only the participants that we are concerned about will be present. Up and until the time of the meeting, if it occurs, we do not believe that the participants will appear to you and your staff or anyone else as anything other than convention-goers."

"We have a list of names here," said Mike, addressing his questions to Sue Kermis. "These people, so far as we know, recently joined the Virtual Parrot Head Club and are using that membership as a guise to come to the convention to conduct this meeting with other individuals we cannot name. All that we ask is that you contact us if and when these people register."

"Also," said Jake, "we have undercover operatives who have also become members of various Parrothead clubs throughout the country and will be in attendance. Again, these people will take no action whatsoever during any convention activities. Once we know the location of a meeting, they will make preparations to be in place to obtain custody of the participants of that meeting, removed from the activities of your membership."

David Cohen spoke up.

"Excuse me, Mr. Sullivan, I don't mean to interrupt you, but you know you can't guarantee that will happen. What if one of these guys decides to put up a fight and it spills over into where our membership is having an activity? Are you trying to tell me that harm couldn't come to any of these people?"

"All I can tell you, Mr. Cohen, is that we are taking every step available to us to ensure that doesn't happen. Can we say with absolute certainty that something like that cannot happen? No, we can't. However, we will say that its likelihood is extremely minimal due to the precautions we are taking. I'm sorry I can't tell you more. National security prevents us from doing so. All we can say is that these men belong to an organization that poses a severe threat to this country, and this is our only opportunity to seize the top operatives of that organization in one setting. Mike and I will personally be available to you at any time. We are giving all of you our cards with numbers to encrypted devices in our possession. If you enter those numbers into your cell phones, your calls will be scrambled and come only to us, and no one will know where those calls are coming from or what is being said . . . so if you see or hear anything that alarms you, concerns you, or if you have any information you can pass on to us at any time concerning these men or this meeting, we would appreciate it. We will have people on site throughout your entire convention to not only assist in apprehending these individuals, but protecting your membership."

Talbert looked around at the Board members.

"Anyone have anything they want to say? Any questions?"

"We don't have much of a choice," said Fyffe. "We can't cancel it now."

"Looks like we're in," said Talbert, "whether we want to be or not. Just make sure our membership is safe, Jake."

"We will," said Jake. "You have my word."

Talbert looked at his Board members again.

"That's always been good enough in the past. Let's hope it is this time, too."

"One other thing," said Mike, "you've all been vetted, and we feel obligated and capable of providing you with the information we have today because of that vetting. You have to understand that the group we are dealing with has inroads in practically every aspect of this country's activities, and other countries around the world, for that matter. We can't be sure that there aren't other people who have infiltrated your organization, so we would ask that what has been said here remains with you six and no one else."

"That goes without saying," said Talbert. He looked at the rest of the Board. "You heard the man . . . anyone have any objections?"

Looking at each other and looking back at Talbert, they all shook their heads in the negative.

"Again," said Jake, standing up and ending the meeting, "if you see anything that concerns you, anything at all, no matter how trivial, call us. It could be significant."

"Communications are key in this thing, folks," said Mike. "We appreciate any help you can give us, and we'll take care of your people."

"That's it then," said Talbert, standing and holding out his hand to Jake and then Mike. "Anything else you need us to do prior to the convention starting?"

"I'm afraid not, Andrew," said Jake. "We're all in the same boat. All we can do now is wait."

THE
WAIT

CHAPTER 41

Jake became irritated. He felt anxiety and unease as he remembered the waiting.

And wait they did. Walsh was doing everything he could, tying-in to all the technology that FSI provided, checking chatter, reservations, and everything else at his disposal, but there was no further information to be had.

The only good news was that during a conversation Jake had with Linda about the girls, he thought he could feel the ice starting to melt somewhat, and they seemed to have a normal conversation. Jake was careful not to bring up anything about the work he was doing and neither did Linda, and they talked about getting together for the holidays back in Pennsylvania.

Mike had gone home the first weekend in October and was going to bring Charlie down to Key West with him, as she had some vacation time coming from the Smithsonian.

Jake kept busy reviewing all the data coming in and issuing orders to the offices throughout the agency, giving reports to Fletcher and holding daily briefings with Walsh.

And then it happened.

Around the third week of October, after Mike had returned with Charlie and taken up residence at the Pier House, Walsh finally had something.

It was early morning on a Tuesday, a week before Meeting Of The Minds was supposed to begin, and Mike and Jake were in his office going over reports, when Walsh rapped on the door jam.

"I think I've finally got something."

"Don't keep us in suspense," said Mike. "What is it?"

Walsh moved into the office and took his normal seat at the left of Jake's desk.

"I came across some chatter. Looks like it originated in Albania, but I can't be sure. It's talking about a party and a celebration with very important guests. It passes itself off as being a family event."

"And what makes you think it isn't?" asked Jake.

"Because it's talking about a party because of someone's promotion. It goes on to say that the promotion will give this person something important."

"And?" said Mike.

"Well, the word they use to mean something important is 'celes'."

"Sam, you're killing me. What are you getting at?" said Jake.

"'Celes' is really translated in Albanian to mean 'key' or 'keys' and the ending uses the word 'besa', which means something very significant, like word of honor or faith. So, maybe something significant is happening and the whole significant word in the thing is 'keys' . . . such as the Florida Keys . . . where maybe someone is being promoted . . . I don't know. The language just doesn't seem to be the normal flow of someone who is talking about a family gathering."

Mike sat back, rubbing his chin.

"Certainly not conclusive," he said, looking at Jake.

"No, but it sort of fits in with what we've been thinking. All right, Sam, thanks. See if you can narrow it down and give us anything else."

"Will do," said Walsh, turning and preparing to exit.

"And, Sam," said Jake.

"Yeah?" said Walsh, turning around.

"Get some sleep."

"Yeah, yeah, I know," said Walsh as he headed out the door.

THE PADRE ALMIRANTE

CHAPTER 42

It was the end of the week before Meeting Of The Minds before Sam Walsh found anything else. This time it was early evening, and this time he entered Jake's office without knocking.

"This could be it," he said. "It's strange the way it's phrased, but it could be it."

"Let's have it," said Jake, looking at Mike.

"Okay, this one's in Spanish, allegedly originating somewhere on the Iberian Peninsula, but I was able to trace it through at least a couple of towers, and I noticed some ping-ponging between a tower on the north shore of Cuba and one in Barcelona. I can't say the origination point was Cuba, but the signal definitely went there on its travels. It's just a two-word phrase. 'Padre Almirante'."

"Padre? That's father, isn't it?" asked Mike.

"Could be father," said Walsh. "Father figure, leader, person of importance . . ."

"What about the second word?" said Jake.

"It usually means admiral."

"Admiral?" said Mike. "What the hell's 'admiral' have to do with this thing?"

"Let's think about this a minute," said Jake, getting up and walking around. "Let's assume just for a minute that 'padre' refers to Ortiz. There's nothing else at all?" asked Jake, looking at Walsh.

"Nothing that makes any sense. I don't even know if this phrase goes with the other phrase, Jake," said Sam.

"All right, we'll figure it out. What is it?"

"The best I can make out is it means 'we will sell the goods on the island' – that's roughly, because the words don't format correctly."

"All right. Let's take it as is," said Jake, writing everything on the white board that had been set up. "So, we have 'padre' and 'almirante' and something that could mean 'we will sell the goods on the island'."

"I'm not seeing it," said Mike, staring at the board.

"Give it some time," said Jake, "give it some time. What if," said Jake, tapping a marker on his desk, "what if sell isn't s-e-l-l, but sail, s-a-i-l? The leader being the goods who will sail to the island. Admiral – a person who runs a boat."

"Ortiz is being brought to Key West by boat?" asked Mike.

"Exactly," said Jake. "Maybe. What do you think, Sam?"

"I mean, it could be. The admiral part is what bothers me. It's so specific."

"Well, it doesn't contradict anything we've heard of. We already have the Coast Guard notified and in place to watch for any traffic from Cuba trying to enter Key West waters, so it doesn't change anything we're doing, that's for sure."

"Just keep it up there," said Mike. "Maybe we'll come up with something else."

"Sorry, guys. There's nothing else out there. That's all I've heard."

"No, it's good work, Sam," said Jake. "Keep at it, and anything you get, bring to us and we'll see what we have."

THE
CASA

CHAPTER 43

Finally, the day arrived – Wednesday, November 1st. At any given time, Key West was having some type of party. Fantasy Fest had just ended. The power boat races would be coming, and there were other events throughout the year, but the first weekend in November was when three thousand partying Parrotheads descended upon the island, and even though formal registration would be tomorrow morning, many would be arriving today.

Jake and Mike spent the morning working the phones, Jake talking with Andrew Talbert and Mike with the folks at the Casa Marina. Talbert had informed Jake that nothing had really changed, and they had no further information and once again reminded Jake of his promise to keep those in attendance safe.

Jake also took a call that morning from Mark Friedman, President of the Trop Rock Music Association.

"Hi, Mark. Haven't spoken to you in a while," said Jake. He could immediately sense a concern in Friedman's voice.

"Jake, it's my understanding that there are some security issues this year that seem a little bit above normal relative to Meeting Of The Minds. Have you heard anything about that?"

Jake hated the thought of lying to someone he knew so well, but he also knew he had to stick to the plan.

"No, I haven't heard anything like that, Mark, but you know, I'm not really involved in that situation."

"So, you don't know anything about extra security being put in place?"

"No, haven't heard a thing," said Jake, telling the truth as to that aspect of the conversation.

"Would you do me a favor and keep me posted if you find out anything?"

"Be happy to, Mark. How's everything look for the awards show?"

"I think it's going to be a great one this year. A lot of great performers . . . a lot of great music."

"Glad to hear it. And like I said, if I find out anything, I'll let you know."

"Thanks, Jake. Keep in touch."

Jake ended the call and threw his pen across his desk, knowing there was going to be some explaining he would have to do to a person he truly liked and admired, about keeping him in the dark about the events of this weekend.

Standing up, he could sense the agitation in Mike's voice as he continued to speak.

"I'm telling you, you're making a mistake. All that's going to do is draw attention to things. I understand that, but we have the situation under control. Yes. I know. Respectfully, this isn't a situation where your lawyers should be making decisions. Sure. Yeah . . . you, too. Bye. Have a nice day my ass," said Mike.

"What is it?"

"People at the Casa Marina just decided to hire their own separate security force to patrol the event."

"What?!" said Jake, slamming a handful of papers down on the desk. "This is what Friedman was talking about. The President told us he had this under control. His old buddy is a head honcho at Waldorf-Astoria and is supposed to keep the Casa in line! Shit!!"

"Yeah, my sentiments exactly."

"They'll tip them off!"

"That's what I was trying to tell this genius, but lawyers in corporate are concerned about their liability." Jake got up, put his hands on his hips, and again began walking around the office.

"It gets better," said Mike.

"Why, what else do you have to tell me?" asked Jake, stopping in mid stride.

"I have a feeling we're going to know very soon..."

Just then, Eva came through on speaker.

"Jake . . . Mike . . . there's an old friend here to see you."

"Send him in," said Mike.

Jake looked at him and raised his hands as if to say, "How do you know who this is?" when Lester Kirkland strode through the door. Jake looked at Mike.

"You've got to be kidding me."

"Meet the Head of Security for the Meeting Of The Minds at the Casa Marina," said Mike.

"Don't look so shocked, Jake. My reputation precedes me," he said, slapping Mike on the back as he took a seat beside his desk.

"Lester, you know what's going on here?" asked Jake, sitting down.

"I have some idea. Actually, I have a very good idea, I think. You two have some type of information to lead you to believe there's going to be a very significant meeting of some very bad people under the cover of this Parrothead thing over at the Casa, and you're keeping everything under wraps because they don't know you know, and you're going to try and tie this whole thing up with one big bow. Am I close?"

"Close enough," said Mike.

"I'm only here to help, boys."

"Yeah, how well did that go last time?" asked Jake.

"Hey, hey . . . that thing wasn't on me. No one could expect that lady to do what she did."

"Let's just say I have my doubts about that," said Jake, taking a seat. "Listen, Les, we can't tip these people off."

"I know, Jake, I know. Hey, how long have I been working in this business?"

"You were Attorney General, Lester."

"Listen, when you have to deal with as many congressional committees as I have and get the briefings I've gotten, I know just as much as you do regarding these situations. Everybody I'm using is undercover, just like the people you have there, I'm sure. Nobody's going to stick out. Brought them all in from other areas. No ties to the island. Everything's going to be fine. It's just that if something happens, you're going to have more back-up than you had before. That's it. Otherwise, it's your show. I don't want to know anything else. We're good."

"Les, we go back a long way, but let me tell you one thing . . . if this thing gets blown, I'm coming after you."

"Geez," said Kirkland, looking at Mike, "what'd he do . . . get up on the wrong side of the bed this morning?"

"I don't think he's kidding," said Mike.

"What? You, too?"

Mike just shrugged.

"All right, seems like a good time for me to leave. As I said, if you need anything, you know how to reach me," and he was gone.

"It's all right, Jake," said Mike. "Maybe he'll be an asset."

"And when has that ever happened?" asked Jake, as he stood up and said, "All right, that's enough. Come on. We're going to go take a stroll around the island. It' a beautiful day. We're supposed to be acting normal. Normal in Key West means taking a stroll along Duval. And just so the normalcy extends into the evening, I've made dinner reservations for you, Charlie, and myself at Louie's"

"Now that sounds like a plan," said Mike, rising and joining him. "Charlie will love that place."

"I think she will," said Jake, and then softly, "Linda always did. Eva," said Jake as he passed her desk, "we're going out to take a stroll down Duval. Get hold of us if anything happens or if you need us for anything."

They were almost out the door when he said, "I'm forgetting the most important thing," and Mike looked at him quizzically. He walked back to the tech room and stuck his head in the door. "Sam, use your portable. Let's go. Time to go out for a while."

"Really?" asked Walsh.

"Really. Let's go."

"Trust me . . . you don't have to ask me twice. I feel like I live in this room."

"Dangerous times," said Jake. "Dangerous times."

And Walsh joined them as they headed out into the bright Key West sun.

THE ISLAND — REVISITED

CHAPTER 44

Jake could hear the noises and feel the warmth of the sun, as he moved to the next scene in his never-ending movie.

The streets were already a little more crowded. There was no cruise ship in town, but there appeared to be more floral shirts and other decorations and a lot of people wearing t-shirts with Jimmy Buffett song titles and lyrics and other paraphernalia. It looked like, at least in part, the Parrotheads had arrived.

It was a beautiful day . . . clear blue sky, nice wind coming in off the Gulf, palm trees green and swaying . . . all seemed right with the world as Jake lead his friends and headed down Whitehead to Eaton, then made a right on Duval. They went past the La Concha and Margaritaville. The window onto the street was open as the early afternoon crowd had significantly increased with the arrival of the Phlock.

"Looks like they've arrived," said Mike.

"Indeed they have. Looks like everybody's having a good time so far," said Jake.

"They don't know what we do," said Walsh.

"Hey," said Mike, "look at the day. No negativity."

"Uh huh," said Walsh.

They were in front of the San Carlos Theater when Jake noticed the van from which people were emptying musical instruments and equipment. A huge smile spread over his face as he walked up and tapped a man with a straw hat, and what appeared to be dreadlocks, on the back. At the same moment, another man and woman came out of the theater and approached where they were standing. The man with the straw hat turned around and spoke first.

"Jake! How the hell you been?! It's been too long, man!"

"I know Donny. I see you're still hanging out with the wrong people," and Jake stuck out his hand. "Eric, how are you?"

"Good, Jake. Yourself?"

Jake continued past him and hugged the woman standing beside them with blonde hair.

"You haven't gotten rid of this guy yet, Gina?"

"So far, he's been doing all right, Jake. I'll keep him for a while," she said, and they all laughed.

"Where's Michelle?"

Another woman popped her head out from the van that Donny had been emptying.

"Here as usual, Jake, doing the dirty work."

She stepped out of the van and gave Jake a hug. It wasn't until then that Jake noticed Mike and Sam standing there, slack-jawed, wondering what the hell was going on.

"Excuse my manners. Donny and Michelle Brewer, Eric and Gina Babin, meet Mike Lang and Sam Walsh. These guys work with me. Donny is one of the best musicians in the business, and this is his wife, Michelle. And Eric and Gina run an online radio station, Radio Trop Rock, one of the fastest growing trop rock radio stations in the country."

As Mike and Sam shook everyone's hands, Jake continued.

"Ready for the show tonight?"

"Absolutely," said Donny. "You going to stop by?"

"Have to see how the day plays out."

"I know you're in the private sector now, buddy. Seems like you're still playing government agent."

"No . . . just working on a couple of things . . . nothing important."

"Well, if you get a chance, stop by. I've got a new song I'm going to perform . . . and you'll love it . . . it's about bad guys in the tropics."

"I promise, I'll make it if I can. You all take care."

Everyone then said their goodbyes and began lugging equipment into the theater.

CHAPTER 45

They then proceeded down Duval until Applerouth Lane, where Jake made a right and then stopped in front of a white stucco building with glass block windows and black bar stools out front and a neon sign indicating it was "Mary Ellen's Bar". Jake led the way inside and looked around until he saw whom he was looking for. They approached a man and a woman standing near the bar with a table beside them cluttered with equipment. There was a banner hanging on the table that said, "Radio A1A". The man saw Jake coming and pointed and smiled, and the woman turned around. She was wearing a straw hat, sunglasses, and had a drink of some sort in one hand and an unlit cigar in the other. She headed for Jake as soon as she saw him and put her arms around him.

"Jake Sullivan! So good to see you again! It's been a while!"

"Indeed it has, Mayor . . . indeed it has. Please, let me introduce my friends. Mike Lang, Sam Walsh . . . this is Mayor Sammie Mays, affectionately known as Gonzo, the Honorary Mayor of Key West."

The Mayor went up to each of them, took their hands in hers, and welcomed them to her city as only she could, while Jake reached out and shook the hand of the gentleman wearing the A1A baseball cap with a white ponytail coming out the back.

"Harry, good to see you. How you doing, man?"

Harry, who was Harry Teaford, also known as Harry T, the head of Radio A1A, the largest Trop Rock music station in the country, where only independent singer-songwriters performed, took Jake's hand in his.

"Great to see you, Jake. How's everything?"

"All's well."

Jake looked back to where the Mayor was still in animated conversation with Mike and Sam.

"Looks like the Mayor is in rare form."

"You should have been here yesterday," said Harry. "She had her Halloween party. From what I can remember of it, it was a remarkable event."

"They always are, Harry . . . they always are."

"So what brings you out and about?"

"Just a beautiful day. Thought I'd take the boys out and see the town."

"You going to be able to come down Friday night to the event?"

"Don't know yet. I'll make it if I can."

"A lot of good music on that stage."

"I know that. I've got to break these two into the Trop Rock world."

"Well, you're definitely in the right place at the right time," said Harry.

"I'll talk to you later," said Jake, who went back to Mike and Sam. "Mayor, I hate to break this up, but we have to move on."

"These boys haven't even had a drink yet. I know you don't partake, but these two look like they're ready to go."

"Normally, I'd be delighted, but there's just someplace we have to be."

"Too much work, Jake . . . too much work."

"Speaking of work," said Jake, pulling her aside, "you haven't heard of any strange goings on in town, have you?"

"This is Key West, Jake, you have to qualify that a little bit more."

Jake just smiled at her.

"I know, I know. I know what *you* mean. No. I haven't heard anything. Why? Is something going on?"

"Don't think so, but you can never be too sure these days. Any time there's a big gathering of people..."

"I'll keep listening."

"You let me know if you hear anything."

"I will," said the Mayor.

"You and Harry take care."

"Always."

Just then, a group of Parrotheads walked in the door, saw the Mayor, and rushed her away.

"Excuse me, Jake. Got to do my thing."

Jake laughed and ushered Mike and Sam out the door.

"Okay," said Mike, "who was that?"

"That is Sammie Mays. Sammie Mays worked for the *National Inquirer*. I don't know if you remember, but she's the one who broke the story about Pete Rose, one of your heroes. She got the interview while he was in prison that no one else could get."

"I *do* remember that," said Mike.

"She is now the Honorary Mayor of Key West, by official proclamation. She's a writer, investigative journalist, and a damn good woman in my estimation."

"Now, she seems like she would be fun to spend some time with in this town," said Walsh.

"You have no idea," said Jake.

CHAPTER 46

"So where to now?" asked Mike.

"Anybody hungry?"

"I could eat," said Walsh.

"All right, listen. We have to go up to the other end of the island. Got to talk to a friend in the Police Department up on North Roosevelt. We'll stop for lunch at El Siboney, where, in my estimation, there is the best Cuban sandwich on the island, and we'll go see my buddy, Ricardo Alonzo."

"Does he know what's going on?"

"No. Let's just say we share insights from time to time. If he's heard anything, he'll let me know . . . and he won't press me about what I know."

"Sounds like a plan," said Mike. "Let's go eat."

CHAPTER 47

Jake had been true to his word. The Cuban sandwiches were excellent, and they called for a cab and took it to the Key West Police Department on North Roosevelt. Jake had called ahead to make sure Sergeant Alonzo was on duty, and he was waiting for them outside the building, looking toward the Garrison Bight Causeway.

"Uh oh," he said, standing up, reaching out to shake Jake's hand. "You brought help. This can't be anything good."

"Easy, Rick, easy. Everything's fine."

"Then to what do I owe this honor?" said Alonzo, looking out again toward the Bight.

"Just snooping around a little. Hear anything unusual?"

"Unusual? Hell, Jake, we just got done with Fantasy Fest, and now we've got Parrotheads, and then we have the boaters. It's always unusual."

"Come on, Rick, you know what I mean."

"What are you sniffing around about? And why do you have your tech guy out and about, and your buddy, Mike Lang, down here from headquarters?"

"See, I told you he knows everything. I didn't even have to introduce you."

"Lang, you made the papers enough for me to know who you are, and I know *everybody* that's on this island, and that includes Mr. Walsh here."

"Like I said, Rick, just doing a little snooping. That's what I do now."

"Uh huh," said Alonzo. "Well, if your snooping leads to anything, I better be the first to hear it. I don't want any surprises."

"Come on, Rick. Anything?"

"No. Nothing out of the ordinary. Just the usual craziness."

"Will you let me know if you do?"

"Will you let me know if *you* do?"

"Rick, I'm always up front with you, as much as I can be."

"Yeah, I love how you always qualify that remark."

Jake just stared at him.

"Don't worry. If I hear anything, I'll let you know. Other than that, please leave my island in one piece."

"Wow, Jake, what have you done here?"

"It's you two together," said Alonzo, pointing at Mike, "that worry me."

"See," said Jake to Mike, "I always knew you were the trouble maker."

"Thanks, Rick."

"Yeah, yeah," and Alonzo turned and headed back toward the building.

As they were walking away, they heard him.

"Hey Lang!"
"Yeah?"
"Take care of him, will you?"
"Always," said Mike. "See, he knows how this really works."
"Whatever you say, Mike. Whatever you say."

CHAPTER 48

They then took a cab back to the FSI office and spent the rest of the afternoon trying to see if they could find out more about the father, the admiral, the party, and the meeting.

It was early evening when they finally called it quits. Walsh had nothing more to report, and Jake and Mike had come to no more conclusions.

"All right, let's call it a night and hit it early tomorrow," said Jake.

"I could sleep for a week," said Walsh, as he left the offices.

"When this is all over, you can," said Jake, "but tomorrow morning . . ."

"I know, I know," said Sam, "I'll be here early. Don't worry."

After he had gone, Mike looked at Jake.

"If I know that kid, he'll be working on this tonight."

"Probably," said Jake.

"All right. I'm going to head down to the Pier House and see if I can drag Charlie off the beach and get ready for dinner. You want us to pick you up?"

"Yeah, that'd be great," said Jake. "The Z-4 is a little crowded for three."

CHAPTER 49

Mike and Charlie pulled up in a rental provided by FSI at 7:00 o'clock on the dot, and Jake came down and got in, and they headed down Whitehead to Eaton and onto Duval to the Atlantic side of the island.

They were lucky enough to find a parking space on Waddell, and Jake led them along the side of Louie's to the iron gate that led to the Afterdeck. He directed them to the bar while he went up the steps on the terrace to confirm their reservation and was soon sitting back at the bar beside them.

"Margaritas I see."

"This place is beautiful," said Charlie.

"Seemed fitting," said Jake. "You're right."

The terrace lights had come on and the sky started to show early stains of indigo spreading out to the horizon.

Jake ordered a Diet Coke and offered a toast.

"To two of my favorite people."

"Back at ya, buddy," said Mike.

Charlie just smiled, hugged Jake, and kissed him on the cheek.

Just then, Mike eyed a waiter.

"Looks like dinner's ready. Let's go eat."

Dinner was a respite from all their investigations and what might transpire the remainder of the week. Mike and Charlie told a hilarious story of Mike's embarrassment when a lady clad only in body paint sat down on the bar stool next to him at the Chart Room, where he and Charlie had gone for a late-night drink a few days previous during Fantasy Fest, and then Jake and Mike told Charlie about the time when Mike was still with the FBI and he had come down to help Jake when Matthews and another Ortiz were after him, and they had sat out at the beach bar at the Pier House where they missed every clue imaginable and said everything the wrong way to enforce a lady's belief that they were gay rather than friends.

"You know, Jake, I have to tell you something. Walking down Duval Street today and listening to all the music coming out of the bars and meeting all the people you introduced me to, I think I'm beginning to understand a little bit about this trop rock/parrothead thing." He looked at Charlie.

"Go ahead," she said. "Tell him."

"Tell me what?" asked Jake.

"That first weekend in October when I went home to see Charlie, she dragged me to Annapolis. It was a beautiful fall day. We were walking around the old part of town, and then we went down to the dock. There was a boat show going on, and there was a guy playing that sang a rendition of *Southern Cross* that was just unbelievable. And I later found out that he was . . ."

Jake interrupted, "Eric Stone. A Trop Rock singer-songwriter and a great talent."

"Exactly," said Mike. "I'm really starting to get it."

"I would hope so, Mike," said Jake, "you're in Key West during MOTM. There's no better place or time."

"I know, I know . . . but we're busy here. I just wanted you to know that I can adapt to new things."

"Sure you can," said Jake, laughing. "Thanks, Charlie. I appreciate the effort."

They told more stories, they laughed, they relaxed, and the night was too short. Before he knew it, Jake was saying goodbye and getting out of the car and heading to his apartment.

As he was moving toward the building, he caught a glimmer of a light in the area of the offices where Sam's tech center was located. Quietly, he approached the office door and slid open a panel that only he knew about and removed a Glock and tried the door handle. It wasn't locked, and he entered. He could see the light coming out from the closed door to Sam's office and slowly moved toward the door. He put his hand gently on the handle, raised the Glock up in front of him, and pushed it open, shouting, "Don't move!" as he entered.

A startled Hector Sanchez, the office handyman, stared back at him, mouth agape, and his eyes focused on the gun, which Jake quickly put behind him.

"Hector, what the hell are you doing here?" A stupid question, as he saw Hector's cleaning supplies beside him.

"Everybody's been in the offices all the time during the day. I came to clean."

Jake looked at the spray bottle in Hector's one hand and the rag in the other, looked at the pail again, and apologized.

"Sorry, Hector, just a little jumpy these days, I guess. Are you almost done, or are you just starting?"

"No, no. Everything out there is done. I'm done. I'm leaving."

"Sorry about this, Hector," he said to his back as he was heading out of Sam's office.

As usual with Hector, there was no reply . . . just a negative shaking of the head, as he made his way to the front door and out. Jake went behind him and waited until he drove away, then opened the door, made sure no one was on the street, slid open the panel once again, and replaced the Glock.

Similar hiding places had been designed all through the interior and exterior of the building as part of the elaborate security system that had been installed. Jake locked the front door behind him and headed toward the interior stairway that led to his apartment. He went to the refrigerator, took out another can of Diet Coke, and plopped onto the couch and turned on the television.

THE REALIZATION

CHAPTER 50

Up to this point, all the scenes in Key West, all the actions with Mike and Sam, and all the discoveries they had made had rolled past Jake scene after scene, but now he was overcome by darkness. It was as if a thought was trying to pierce through but couldn't quite reach him. It was a thought he knew he had to hold on to.
"I'm missing something ... something important ..."and then he remembered the other movie.

Jake awoke with a start and sat bolt upright on the couch. He shook his head, realizing he was sitting in his own apartment, and he looked at his watch. He had fallen asleep and had slept for almost an hour. The movie was still playing on the television and he sat back and took a swig from the Diet Coke on the end table beside him and turned up the volume. He smiled to himself as the old movie with its well-known actors played on. "Knute Rockne – All American" – one of Jake's favorites when he was young – Pat O'Brien was Rockne, Donald Crisp was Father John Callahan, and President to be Ronald Reagan was George Gipp – the Gipper.

The scene before him was a famous one where Rockne is explaining that he wants to be a coach and not a scientist to Crisp, and the good Father encourages him to do what he must, assuring him that he will be good at whatever he chooses.

And then it happened, as it did so often with Jake, first it was just a small, small thought in the back of his mind, a sense of something. He pressed rewind on the remote and let the scene play again, and he started to think it through, and the small, nagging thought became an idea. And as he played things back and forth in his mind, it grew to an almost certainty, but Jake knew he had to explore it further to make sure.

Little sleep came to him that night as he replayed the scene in the movie and continued to put pieces of the puzzle together in his mind and to determine what else he needed to do.

CHAPTER 51

Jake was in the office early. If he couldn't sleep, he might as well get some work done.

As usual, Eva and Sam Walsh arrived together, well ahead of when they had to be there, and Jake came out to meet them.

"Jake, you look terrible," said Eva.

"Good morning to you, too," said Jake.

"No, seriously, did you spend another night working?"

"No, I was up in my apartment watching a movie."

"A movie?" said Eva.

"Yeah, one of my favorites about Knute Rockne."

Eva looked at him suspiciously.

"And?"

"That's all. Just a movie. Sam, come on in, I want to talk to you about something." Pushing the door closed, he looked at Walsh. "Listen, do me a favor. Check something out on this. I pulled these two incidents out of the database. One involved a Saudi businessman in Riyadh and the other a CIA Station Chief in Jerusalem. There were some bystanders killed in each situation, and I want to know if any of those individuals had any type of significance . . . what they were doing there, where they were from . . . complete rundown, all right?"

"Yeah, sure, I can do that."

"I need it fast, and I need one more thing, and, Sam, all this is between only you and me. Not Mike, not anyone else, you understand?"

"Okay."

"I want to know the highest rank this man achieved in the Navy."

Sam looked at the name and back at Jake.

"Jake, what's going on?"

"I'm not sure yet, and I need this information to find out."

"You don't think . . ."

"Sam, I told you all I can tell you. Get me the information as soon as you can."

Sam looked at the name once more and handed the paper back to Jake.

"I'm on it," and he left the office.

Jake buzzed Eva.

"All right, young lady, come on in . . . let's go over what we have today."

CHAPTER 52

Jake chewed on his idea the rest of the day, and finally, he made a call to Jason Bates.

"Jason, I need a little bit of information if you can help me."

"Make it quick, Sullivan, we're busy here, too, you know."

"Was there any group of people or any individual who was really pushing the President in selecting Jason Adams for Vice President?"

"No. He discussed it with a lot of people, Sullivan. I don't think I can pinpoint anybody. Why are you asking?"

"Just checking out a couple of things."

"Hold on a second. Let me check the phone calls for that period." After a minute or so, Bates was back. "Okay, here's the list," and he read off a list of names.

"Thanks, Jason, I appreciate your time."

"Yeah, yeah," came the reply from Bates as he hung up.

"*Another piece to the puzzle,*" thought Jake. He was almost there.

No word came in from any sources as to the scheduling of a meeting or the arrival of any of the five holding the aliases that had joined the Virtual Parrot Head Club, and none of them had attempted registration.

Thursday night into Friday, and it was more of the same until mid-afternoon, when Jake took a call from Rick Fyffe, Head of Registration, which he put on speaker.

"All five registered late and at approximately the same time, and one of them reserved a meeting room at the Casa Marina."

Jake could fill the adrenaline rushing through him.

"When is the meeting scheduled for?"

"9:00 P.M., in Meeting Room 3."

"Thanks Rick. Keep me posted if anything changes."

"Will do."

"And Rick, listen, do you have anything at all scheduled around that meeting room area tonight?"

"No. Everything is out on the beach tonight, Jake. Tonight's the award show."

"All right," said Jake, "thanks."

"That figures," he said to Mike. "It's Friday. The awards ceremony is tonight. There will be a lot of action going on with a large crowd. Nobody will be anywhere near that meeting room, but all the people give them good cover for their comings and goings."

Mike and Jake began notifications to all the agencies and operations involved. The meeting room was put under surveillance with visual and audio, and more undercover operatives were put into the crowd, with photos of the five to see if they could locate any or all of them.

The plan was that since Jake and Mike were so well known to Group 45's operatives and leadership group, Jake would set up outside in an unmarked vehicle to see if they could catch Ortiz entering the premises, and also to make sure that if anyone somehow alluded the undercover operatives, they could stop any attempt to escape. It was decided that Mike would work from the office and coordinate the undercover operation inside the Casa while Jake established the outside perimeter.

CHAPTER 53

Jake was pacing back and forth and Mike was still studying information coming in on his computer when Walsh knocked on the door jam.

"Jake, I need to show you something."

Jake looked over at Mike, who waved him off, and Jake headed out of the office, following Walsh.

"What have you got, Sam?"

"That request you gave me . . . the event in Riyadh . . . one of the bystanders who was killed was an Arab negotiator from Yemen, who was there to meet with the Saudis. In Jerusalem, one of the victims was the leader of an Israeli opposition party, who was there to try and start peace talks with the Palestinians."

"And what about rank?"

"Jake, where are you going with this?"

"Just answer the question, Sam. What was the rank?"

"O-7."

Jake turned and looked back at Sam.

"Rear admiral. One star. Lower half."

"That's right."

"Thanks, Sam."

"Jake . . ."

"That's all I can tell you right now, Sam. I'm playing a hunch. I'll keep you posted."

"Anything else I can do?" asked Walsh.

"Just keep doing what you're doing. I appreciate everything you do. Tonight's the night."

Walsh looked long and hard at Jake.

"I hope to God you're wrong. You know it could be a trap."

"So do I," said Jake, "but I'm not. And yes, I know."

THE NIGHT

CHAPTER 54

The scenes continued to come and go in front of Jake. There was the occasional voice and shadow above him, and then there was silence and everything was still and dark. He remembered the darkness . . . the darkness of that night, and he realized he was sweating, and he began to feel the cold and the wetness, and then the scenes appeared again . . .

The hours moved slowly toward 9:00 o'clock as Mike and Walsh manned the screens in the office and coordinated the search inside for the leaders of Group 45. Jake had taken up position in a van on the corner of White and Casa Marina Court, where he could see the front and side entrances to the resort.

A light rain had started earlier in the day and had grown heavy as the night progressed. Jake knew it didn't matter. The crowd would still be going crazy inside as the musical event would go on, rain or no rain. 9:00 o'clock approached and still no word from the operatives.

Finally, it came across Jake's ear set.

"This is Denault. We might have something. Just hold on."

Jake contacted the other members of the outside coordination team. And then everything happened at once. The call came across the headsets of all the parties involved.

"Jake! It's a trick! It's all a decoy! There's no one here!"

And the call set in motion a series of events. Mike bolted from the office, telling Walsh to make sure everyone stayed in contact as he headed to the Casa to double check what had been found. The operatives spread out to try to clear all of the escape routes, and Jake stood on the corner of White and Casa Marina Court in the pouring rain, knowing they had been fooled all along.

CHAPTER 55

Indeed it was a decoy, as Antonio Ortiz had met with the five leaders of Group 45 and was unanimously elected the Leader at his seaside villa a week earlier.

They had all arrived in Cuba by boat or plane from Mexico and Canada – all under assumed identities never before used and not on any agency's radar.

The only use of the prior known aliases registered for the convention was when five subordinates signed in at the Casa. Thereafter, they immediately slipped into the crowd and made their ways to various exits and left the resort. They made their separate ways to a bed and breakfast that had been leased in its entirety by one of their compatriots in Key West until they were transported off the island.

Ortiz, himself, had flown in on the private jet of a certain Miami businessman who was part of their cause and had traveled south down U.S. 1 disguised as a tourist, his supposed wife a member of the organization.

Upon reaching Key West, Ortiz took up residence in the home of the compatriot who had rented the bed and breakfast for the others. He had a perfectly copied identification tag on a hideously garish lanyard and went into the Casa Marina this night only in the appropriate floral shirt, straw hat, and flip flops.

The guards at the doorway had glanced at his identification tag and waved him through, telling him to enjoy himself and have a great time. Out of an abundance of caution, he had gone straight into the basement and changed into the uniform of a repairman, showing he was an employee of Ralston Air Conditioning Company, the same name on a van that awaited him at the side entrance to the hotel. And while the other five had already left the island, it was Ortiz's intention not to . . . not yet. He had obtained the necessary information, and had insisted that he, and he alone, would carry out the final part of the plan.

CHAPTER 56

Jake waited and watched for the final part of the trap to spring. And then came the call.

"Jake! Listen . . . it's Les Kirkland! I think I've just seen Ortiz heading for the side entrance of the hotel! I'm in pursuit!"

Jake checked his Glock. He started walking slowly down the street to the side entrance. As he did, he saw two men exit the door. One appeared to be dressed in casual clothes, and the other one was wearing a tool belt and a worker's uniform. Jake watched as he went to the back of the van with lettering on it that Jake couldn't quite make out and opened it and put a toolbox inside. Jake raised his Glock. The man had limped the whole way, and now he slowly turned and limped several paces forward toward Jake until he was under a street light and smiled. The recognition was instantaneous, and Jake leveled his weapon.

Just then, a black SUV came barreling down past him and pulled in sideways, cutting off Jake's view of the van and the man he knew was Antonio Ortiz. He heard doors open and close and then it slammed into reverse, then forward, and headed down the street. Jake watched the SUV speed off and make a right onto Reynolds, Ortiz and the other man both gone.

"*I'm going to lose him,*" he thought, knowing they were heading for Duval, as he looked back toward the corner where the communications van was parked, and he knew he didn't have time. He knew who the other man was, and that it was a trap, but he had to follow them.

Just then, a tourist kid on a scooter, his girlfriend behind him, both of them wearing ponchos as protection against the rain, which had slowed to a drizzle, made the turn from White and approached him. Jake jumped out in the middle of the street, flashing his old federal badge.

"Federal officer! Sorry, there's a crime in progress! I need your scooter!"

"What the hell?" said the kid, and Jake put his finger right in the middle of his chest.

"Off!" was all he said, and that's all it took.

"C'mon, Jimmy," said the girl. "Give it to him. You don't want to get involved in this."

"Thanks, miss," said Jake, and he got on and headed off, moving toward the departed SUV.

CHAPTER 57

"Mike! This is Jake! I'm in pursuit of Ortiz. He's in a black SUV heading down Duval and Les Kirkland is with him!"

"What?! What did you say?!"

"It's a long story . . . but Kirkland's been working for Group 45 the whole time!"

"Shit!" said Mike. "All right everybody, you heard him. Let's go! What's the destination, Jake?"

"My best guess . . . Mallory Square. There's probably a boat waiting to take them both to Cuba."

"All right everybody, move it! Mallory Square! You sure about this, Jake?"

"Sure as I can be," he said.

"All right. Listen, pull over. I'm coming. We'll get them together."

"Too late," said Jake, "they've already turned into the alley to get to Mallory. I can't let them get away."

"Jake, don't do this yourself. I'll be there," but there was no response.

CHAPTER 58

Because of the rain, traffic had been thin on Duval, and Jake was able to pick up the SUV two blocks ahead of him and keep it in his sights, wiping the rain away from his face with his sleeve and keeping the scooter from skidding in the puddles that had formed on Duval. Jake dropped the scooter just outside of El Meson de Pepe, drew his weapon, and ran down the outside patio of the restaurant into Mallory Square, where he saw the SUV was parked. He stopped to crouch behind a vendor cart and waited for movement.

Just then the front passenger door opened and a man moved around the front of the SUV and went to open the rear door. Jake closed his eyes and shook his head for a moment, wishing that what he had seen wasn't so.

CHAPTER 59

Jake moved out from his hiding place, raised his Glock, and moved toward the SUV.

"Stop right there, Lester! It's over! Or should I call you 'Padre Almirante'?"

Jake noticed that Lester's one hand was down by his side.

"Should have known you'd figure it out, Jake. You always seem to."

"The man who was going to become a priest but went to the Naval Academy instead . . . made it the whole way to an 0-7 . . . rear admiral, lower half . . . a one star . . . and then if I remember correctly, law school at Georgetown."

"Not a bad pedigree, don't you think?" asked Lester, smiling at Jake as he stood in the rain, his hand never leaving his side.

"Not a bad pedigree for a traitor. I checked out those two incidents you were involved in with your security company. That whole thing in Jerusalem . . . you weren't saving the life of the CIA Station Chief . . . you were assassinating the leader of an Israeli opposition party who was there to try and start peace talks with the Palestinians. And that little drama in Riyadh was when you took out an Arab negotiator trying to reset relations with the Saudis. Can't have peace and stability in the world, right Lester? Not Group 45. And, of course, it was you who left the gun in the ladies room at the Pier House. I remember how you waved your man off. And you were one of those pushing Fletcher to pick Adams for Vice President. How long you been in?"

"Quite a while, actually."

"Why? Why'd you do it?"

"Come on, Jake. You know why. What's it matter? It's all a game. It's all bullshit. We're as good or as bad as they are. It's us, Jake. We are the people driving this. We are puppets and they are pulling the strings. Everyone serves a purpose, Jake . . . even you!"

"Don't you dare say I'm the same as you, you son-of-a-bitch!"

"That's it, Jake. Stop. No closer."

Jake, who had been moving forward, shouted out, "You're a traitor, Lester, no matter how you cut it, and I'm here to take you and Ortiz in to pay the price! On your knees Lester . . . now!"

"Maybe it was the sudden gust of wind in his face," thought Jake, as the scene raced through his mind. *"Maybe I was too concentrated on Ortiz. It was just a second. Only a second,"* and then the scene faded.

In the darkness of Mallory Square, Jake did hesitate, and in that second of hesitation, Lester Kirkland raised his weapon and they both fired at the same time.

Jake felt the burning pain as his right shoulder shattered and his Glock fell into the puddle at his feet. As he was falling backwards, he saw Kirkland slide down the side of the SUV, his shirt turning red as a blood stain blossomed.

CHAPTER 60

The pain was increasing. Jake knew the blood loss would lead to unconsciousness. The rain hit his face as his hand searched the puddles, trying to find his weapon, but all he could grasp was the wetness and the cold stones.

The thoughts were coming in a rush to him now. Jake had difficulty sorting them out. What was it? What was there in the center of it all? What was the thing he couldn't remember . . . the thing he needed to know. He winced. He remembered the pain, and he remembered what happened next.

Jake heard the rear door of the SUV open and he lifted his head and saw Antonio Ortiz exiting. He looked past him into the rear seat, illuminated by the overhead light, and then his head fell back and he gasped in pain and in realization, as he listened to the sound of the footsteps as they splashed on the stones in Mallory Square, each step accompanied by the cadence of the tip of the cane on the stones. Then the sounds stopped, and he looked up into the face . . . the face of his enemy, standing over him, smiling.

"I told you, Jake Sullivan . . . I told you I would come for you . . . and here I am . . . and now you will die, and your interference in our business will end."
Jake tried to talk but couldn't, and with his good hand he motioned for Ortiz to come closer.

Ortiz slowly lowered his head, turning his ear toward Jake, and in his last effort, Jake spat in his face.

Ortiz stood up, not angry, but laughing.

"Your final futile gesture, Jake Sullivan," and Ortiz pulled the gun out from the back of his waistband and aimed it at the middle of Jake's forehead. "And now, you die," and he pulled the trigger.

CHAPTER 61

While lying there in the rain, Jake couldn't be sure. Had he heard another shot? There was a new pain and burning in the side of his head, and then there was a shadow above him, and he heard his name . . . far, far away . . . being called . . . a familiar voice . . . and then lights . . . red, then blue and white, flashing . . . and then there was nothing but darkness.

CHAPTER 62

Speeding to the scene, Mike took the same route into the Square as Jake, and he, too, crouched down behind one of the vendor carts and saw a man with a gun standing over a man lying on his back. He saw the man raise the gun and point it, and instinctively, he pulled out his own weapon and fired, and the man jerked just as Mike saw the flash from his weapon. He saw the man stagger. He had hit him, and he shot again, but the man ducked and began to hobble away with his cane.

Just then, two men exited from an SUV that pulled into the Square, firing automatic weapons in Mike's direction. He lunged back behind the vendor cart, and they continued firing until the man limping with the cane had made his way back to the original SUV and entered, and then the men ceased their firing, entered their SUV, and both sped off into the night.

Mike ran through the Square firing his weapon at the exiting vehicles, but to no avail. He saw Lester Kirkland lying dead where the SUVs had been parked, and then he turned and ran to the person lying in the puddles, a person he knew was Jake.

He saw that Jake had been hit in the shoulder and that the side of his head was covered in blood. There was nothing else he could do. He screamed for medics and sat down and took Jake's head and held it in his lap, as the rain continued to fall.

"God damn it, Jake! Why didn't you wait?! I was coming! I was coming! God damn it! Don't you die on me! You hear me!" and the rain mingled with the tears on his cheeks as he sat there in silence, cradling Jake Sullivan's head and rocking back and forth.

EPILOGUE

CHAPTER 63

Mike came to the hospital every night and day as he had for a month, and as he expected, Linda and the girls were still there.

Jake remained unconscious, clinging to life. The neurosurgeons couldn't determine how much brain damage he had sustained by the shot to his head, but they held out hope. His shoulder would be repaired and it would heal, but the rest was something they couldn't guarantee.

"He's strong," said Mike, hugging Linda and the girls. "You know he's strong. He hasn't finished his job yet. He won't let this stop him."

Linda became irate.

"His job did this, Mike! His stupid job that he wouldn't let go! That's what did this!"

"I know," said Mike. "I know, and I couldn't get there when he needed me most."

"It's not your fault, Mike," said all three.

Linda continued, "You know him. He wasn't going to wait for you. He was consumed by putting an end to Group 45. He thought this was his chance to do it, and he took it."

There was silence, and then Mike said again, "He'll get through this. Jake always does."

CHAPTER 64

Another month had passed and Jake had shown no signs of improvement. He still lay there unconscious. The hospital in Miami, where he was a patient, saw a steady stream of experts pass through its doors, as Fletcher spared no expense to get the treatment that Jake needed.

The girls had gone back home. Their real lives required it. There was work, children – things that they had to do.

Linda had taken a leave of absence for the remainder of the semester and was staying in an apartment she had leased near the hospital. She came to visit Jake every day, as did Mike.

But finally, Mike made a decision, and he went back to Washington. He entered Fletcher's office at FSI headquarters.

Fletcher looked up from his desk.

"Any news from Miami?"

"Still unconscious. No movement. Starting to breathe on his own, but nothing else."

"He's tough, Mike. You know that. You're both tough."

"I don't know about this one. I'll need to take some time off."

Fletcher looked at him long and hard.

"I presume you're planning a trip."

"It's probably better you don't know my plans, sir."

"I'll do everything I can to help you, but you know if it goes wrong . . ."

"I know, sir. This is on me . . . but I have to do this . . . for Jake . . . and I'm going to. If you need my resignation, you'll have it."

"No need," said Fletcher.

Mike moved toward the door.

"There's one more thing you need to know, sir," he said without looking back.

"What's that?"

"I'm not bringing him back with me."

And he opened the door and let it shut behind him.

COMING SPRING 2019

CHIP BELL

1725 FIFTH AVENUE
ARNOLD, PA 15068

724-339-2355

chip.bell.author@gmail.com
clb.bcymlaw@verizon.net
www.ChipBellAuthor.com

FOLLOW ME ON FACEBOOK
facebook.com/chipbellauthor

FOLLOW ME ON TWITTER
@ChipBellAuthor

FOLLOW ME ON PINTEREST
pinterest.com/chipbellauthor
/the-jake-sullivan-series

**TAKE THE TIME TO REVIEW
THIS BOOK ON AMAZON**
amazon.com/author
/chipbellauthor.com

Made in the USA
Monee, IL
11 July 2020